Skeemin' On Tha Low

BY: Black Barbie

<u>ACKNOWLEDGEMENTS</u>

I would always give Glory to God, for blessing me with a creative mind-

state.

I would like to thank all of my readers, and fans for all of your support and

encouragement.

Thank you all for supporting, and enjoying your journey into the

imagination of Author Black Barbie.

"Dream It, Believe In It, And Achieve It"

Introduction

It was spring twenty thirteen, late in the evening Friday. Stephanie was in her bedroom, laying across her California king bed bored with herself, trying to figure out what she was going to get herself into later on that night.

Stephanie had begun to flip through random channels on her 60-inch Panasonic flat screen television, in search of something exciting for her to watch seeming that there was nothing else for her to get into currently. Just as Stephanie had begun to get comfortable with herself, she had looked over to notice that her phone was ringing.

Stephanie had sat up on her bed from the lounging position that she was currently in to feel around in between her comforter and sheets, in search of her cellphone. Stephanie continued to fill around trying her best to remember where she had last tossed her cellular-phone before Stephanie had begun watching TV earlier that evening. Although Stephanie was unable to locate her phone right away; she had known from the loud sound of her ring back tone that her cell phone was somewhere close to her bed. Stephanie had begun to feel the music from her ring-back tone, as she continued to search around. Before Stephanie had noticed it, she was twerking and dancing around the head of her bed to her cellphones ring back sound. Stephanie's phone continued to ring louder and louder as she grooved along with the rap song that was blaring in the background, all while still looking through the sheets of her bed and tossing her comforter around.

"Grrr." Stephanie had growled out to herself. "Where in the hell did I put that damn phone," Stephanie mumbled out loud all while starting to get angry and frustrated with herself. Just as she was about to get irritated, Stephanie had noticed that her phone was in between her two big pillows tossed towered the head of her bed. Stephanie was so anxious to find her phone until she had answered it without looking at the caller ID to see who it was calling her on the other end.

Stephanie had recognized the man's voice on the other end of the phone soon as he responded. Stephanie had known that the man on the other end of the phone was submissive and weak-minded towards her every need, and with that being said, Stephanie had begun to think to herself that she was bored and looking forward to having something to get into for the rest of that evening.

Although Stephanie was in an open, committed relationship with her fiancé Mali, they still allowed each other to date other people outside of their relationship, along with strict stipulations on both of their commitment towards each another.

Stephanie would never mention anything about her fiancé Mali to any of the other men that she had dated on the side, nor would she acknowledge the fact that she was engaged and already committed to another man.

Stephanie was secretive and had always kept her personal life private as she would string along with other men that she dated until Mali had decided that it was time for him to come home and dedicate his time to only her whenever he had felt the need to.

"Hello," Stephanie had said to the caller on the other end of her phone while laying back down in her bed to get comfortable again. Before Stephanie could get another word out of her mouth, her male friend on the other end had started talking over her and began taking control of their phone conversation.

"Baby, you know I love you right, I don't want nobody else

but you baby girl, you're all that I need in my life right now, Stephanie." Her male friend had said.

All that had mattered to the man on the other end of the phone that night was that he had Stephanie's full undivided attention. Stephanie, on the other hand, had continued to lay across her bed as he continued to talk to her about a whole bunch of nothing and random jibber jabber, paying him no attention at all. Stephanie had once again found herself flipping through the channels of her TV as her male friend continued to blabber on and on about her not allowing him with an opportunity of being in a committed relationship with him on the other end of the phone. Stephanie had begun to let out a loud sigh as she continued to get comfortable in her bed, bored with his random conversation.

Seeming that her male friend on the other end of the phone was doing the majority of the talking, and never once allowing her to get a single word in. Stephanie had begin to get frustrated with him seeming that they had been on the phone for more than thirty minutes, and hadn't accomplished anything.

Stephanie couldn't figure out where she had gone wrong with this one particular male friend of hers; she thought that she had once made it loud and clear to him the first time that she wasn't interested in him or a relationship with him.

He had already known what Stephanie had said to him previously in the past numerous times before, about being in a relationship. He didn't seem to care about what she had to say; he figured to himself that if he continued to wine and dine her and contribute to her every need, she would eventually one day give in to him. Stephanie's male friend had refused to take no for an answer from her, and one way or another he was going to have her as his leading lady.

Stephanie had met her male friend about eight months ago while she and a few of her girls were out one weekend having drinks at the Hilton Hotel in Oakland.

When Stephanie had first met her male friend, it was right after Christmas in 2012; and her fiancé Mali was out on a so-called business trip with a few of his boys when Stephanie had decided to stay over with her new male friend at his house for a while to get better acquainted with him.

Stephanie decided to get promiscuous with the man that she was now speaking with over the phone because she refused to be alone and by herself in the absence of missing her man Mali. Stephanie hadn't made anything about her private or personal life clear to her male friend at all. Instead, she begins to lead him on just as she had done every other man that crossed her path.

Stephanie's male friend had figured to himself by Stephanie coming over to his house almost every night since they've met, they were beginning to grow into something more with one another than just a friendship. Stephanie's male friend had started to fall in love with her style and with her ways until he had wanted her all to himself.

To Stephanie's friend on the other end of the phone, she was every man and boy's dream; not only was she classy and independent, but she was also street smart and not to add sexy. Stephanie's male friend had never known exactly what it was that Stephanie did for a living, and he never cared to ask how she had made her living.

Unbeknownst to Stephanie's friend, the only real reason she was so comfortable in his downtown Oakland penthouse home was that of the convenience for her to commute to work every day. Stephanie had figured to herself since his loft was close to her job and he hadn't minded her staying over, why not make it easier on herself going back and forth to work whenever.

Stephanie had now been listening to her male friend talk to her over the phone for more than an hour now, as she had begun to find herself nodding off to sleep and reminiscing about the time when they had first meet him.

Stephanie could remember when she had first decided to stay over at his house for a while due to a significant project that she was working on for her to get a new contract with an Atlanta, Georgia television studio. The deadline for her contract was quickly approaching, and it was the beginning of the New Year, she only had one week to get everything finalized and sent in.

Due to the Atlanta contract, Stephanie had found herself working long days and nights due to all of the high demands and negotiations that came along with her new deal. Stephanie had wanted to assure herself that the job was done right the very first time, so she got comfortable with her new male friend and had decided to stay over at his house for a while.

Stephanie could remember leaving her office from working on her project one night. Stephanie had already decided to herself earlier in the day that she didn't want to take the long commute home and deal with all of the traffic and people out partying and celebrating the New Year after work that night. Instead, Stephanie had booked a room and decided to head over to the Marriott Hotel to check in. Just as Stephanie was pulling into valet parking, her cellphone music tone had begun to ring. She had looked at her caller ID to see who was calling her, and noticed that it was her then-new male friend whom she had recently met earlier in the week over at the Hilton Hotel.

Stephanie had a way with men, and if there wasn't anything else she had known how to do, she knew exactly how to read them. Stephanie had noticed that when she first meets her male friend, he was feeling her style so much that he had decided to invite her over to his place to spend some time with him instead of her having to check into a hotel.

Stephanie's male friend had continued to talk to her over the phone nonstop while she continued to flip through the channels all while slightly nodding off and reminiscing about when they had first met. Stephanie was known longer tuned into his conversation; instead, she had wandered off into her daydream.

"So baby girl, what do you have planned for tonight?" Stephanie could remember him asking her with hesitation in his voice over the phone. Stephanie could remember their first conversation as if it was just taking place. Stephanie could remember telling him over the phone back then that she didn't want to intrude on his personal space seeming that this was their very first time speaking with each other since they've met.

Stephanie could remember her male friend finessing her over to his house; he had told her that he wanted to relieve her mind of all of her tension and stress and give her a full body massage. He continued to finesse her into changing her mind about checking into a hotel after work that night by further telling her that he wanted to relax her soul and ease the inside of her body from stress as well. With the offer of a free male sexual full body massage, Stephanie couldn't resist. After nodding off and reminiscing Stephanie had begun to regret ever going over to his house and giving him the time of day ever since.

After the first week of Stephanie staying over with her male friend at his house, he continued begging for her to stay with him a little longer while she completed her work project instead of going home every night. Stephanie could tell her male friend was falling

for her, and she immediately had to let him know then and there

that she wasn't interested in a relationship with him at all. She let

him know that although she enjoyed spending time with him, they

were only sexual friends with no strings or attachments.

　　With Stephanie laying the rules out on the table, it hadn't made

her male friend change his mind about going after her; it didn't

make him go away from her either. Even though Stephanie

demanded not to have a relationship with him, he still catered to

her every need as if she was all his. Stephanie couldn't resist the

attention that he was giving her, so she had decided that she would

continue to stay over with him for a while and continue to be

pampered and showered with gifts. Stephanie's male friend may

have been begging for her attention at that particular moment in

time, but he also had other women asking for his time and attention

as well despite of the attention that he was getting from his female

friends, he was still only interested in Stephanie laying next to him

in bed.

　　Stephanie's friend was a fat, fly guy who had a way with the

woman; and knew how to make every last one of them feel special.

He was so debonair and flamboyant with himself that back when he was in high school, everyone stopped calling him by his legal first name and had started referring to him as The Gentleman. Ever since then, they only knew of him as the Gentleman.

The Gentleman had never been turned down by any woman before, and he refused to let Stephanie be the first to tell him no over and over again.

The Gentleman had stood about five feet ten inches tall, and weighed every bit of 320 pounds. Although he was big and husky, his body fat seemed to fall in all of the right places, which helped him carry his weight well. The Gentleman had always dressed fly, with the latest and greatest gear on that the next big rapper was out there wearing. He made sure that whatever he had on was the fliest gear out at that particular season. The Gentleman had an appearance to himself; wherever he went, someone would always stop him and mistake him for either Cee Lo Green or the gospel singer Marvin Sapp.

The Gentleman was still on the other end of the phone, saying anything and everything that he thought sounded enjoyable and exciting to Stephanie. He always had to work extra hard when it came to getting her full and undivided attention whenever they were on the phone together. He wanted her, and he had found himself turning into somewhat of a stalker.

The Gentleman didn't mind looking foolish or crazy while trying to get Stephanie to agree on being his old lady. In his mind, she was going to be his, and he wasn't going to stop until she was his leading lady and gracefully standing by his side. Stephanie, on the other hand, had no interest in ever being his lady or in a relationship with him at all; that was the least of her worries whenever it came to him.

"Baby girl, you know that I love you," he had said to her once again over the phone, breaking her from her daydream and regaining her undivided attention.

"Hello, Stephanie are you still there?" he had yelled out to her through the phone, now starting to sound upset.

"Yes baby," Stephanie abruptly answered back to him, forgetting who it was that she was on the phone speaking too. "Oops, I meant to say yes, yes I'm listening to you, now what's up again?" Stephanie had rudely blurted out.

The Gentleman had sat on the other end of the phone, eagerly waiting for Stephanie's reply back to all of the campaigning that he was doing for her. He began to also wander off into a daydream of his own with complete silence. He daydreamed of him and Stephanie's future together as a couple. If only he could get, Stephanie to agree with him and be his lady, although she'd turned him down several times before.

Stephanie had always found herself reminding The Gentleman that he was just an option for her, and not someone that she was interested in. She let him know that she wouldn't mind offering him a trip down the friendship zone to remind him of their relationship again.

Stephanie had sometimes taken caution when it came to her choice of words when speaking with other men; she didn't want to mislead anyone on or hurt their feelings intentionally.

The Gentleman on the other end was known different from any of her other sideman that she had dated or dealt with; he had started to seem creepy and demanding to her. Stephanie decided right then and there, that after this phone conversation she was going to cut off all ties with him for good. She had felt that she outgrew him and that she didn't want anything further to do with him at all.

Stephanie had just woke up one weekend no longer interested in the Gentleman. She played it safe by keeping her personal life private, so she never had to worry about him coming to her house or office stalking and looking for her. All the Gentleman knew about her was her first name; he never knew her last name, nor had she ever allowed him to take any pictures with her while they were out in public dating. The only thing The Gentleman knew about Stephanie was where she and her girls hung out at every Friday night, at the Hilton Hotel bar.

One Saturday night while Stephanie and her girls were out having drinks at the Hilton Hotel, The Gentleman popped up unexpectedly out of nowhere and started stalking her and her friends. One of her homegirls was sitting in the middle of the bar flirting with a few of the other men when she had spotted The Gentleman sitting over in the corner by the back of the bar, staring directly at them. He was sipping on a drink while stirring a cocktail straw around in his glass all while staring straight over at Stephanie. Stephanie's homegirl leaned over on her bar stool closer to Stephanie so that she could whisper in her ear.

"Girl you got yourself a little stalker up in here," her homegirl whispered to her while peeking over at The Gentleman at the other end. Stephanie looked up at her girl, intoxicated from drinking, and began to laugh out loud in her face.

"Girl, what in the hell are you talking about child?" Stephanie asked her friend while taking another sip of her pineapple mojito.

"What I'm talking about is that creep, The Gentleman, sitting up over there in the far back of the   bar staring directly at you." Her homegirl had told her while twirling both of their bar stools around so that she could point directly at him.

Stephanie had sat on the phone and continued listening to The Gentleman; she figured to herself this is what she got for being bored at home and desperate for someone to talk to, and answering her phone without ever looking at her caller ID to know that it was him.

Stephanie laid on her bed and dismissed the whole idea of allowing him with an opportunity to treat her out on a date later on that night. Instead, she reminded herself that as soon as he disconnected their call, she was going to restrict his calls and block out his phone number.

Stephanie continued to lay across her bed and daydream with The Gentleman still talking on the other end of the phone when he had finally caught her attention again.

"You old stuck up boogie ass lousy bitch, fuck you!" he had yelled at her through the phone, upset with her for not listening to a word he said to her at all that evening.

Stephanie refused to be bothered with such ignorance or disrespect from any man that she had dealt with. She could never understand how someone could mistake a friendship for a relationship time and time again. Stephanie had known the Gentleman for quite some time, but never once had she led him on to think that their friendship was more than platonic friends. Stephanie didn't care that they were sexually connected with one another, far as she could see, there was no type of physical commitment for them at all to engage in. Stephanie had known that for her to get rid of The Gentleman, she would immediately have to put an end to their friendship.

"So um anyway baby girl, what's up," The Gentleman blurted out to her over the phone, forgetting that he had just tried to curse her out a few seconds ago. "So when can I come wine and dine you again," he had further gone on to ask her.

"I'm cool on you boo boo," Stephanie had told him. She began to get upset with herself at the thought of him having the nerve to ask her to be with him again and again.

"You don't even know me all like that to be on me, and I've never once given you the impression that I wanted to be in a relationship with you. I'm still having a hard time trying to figure out and understand why you would even be bold enough to ask me something like that," Stephanie had said as she caught herself once again reminding The Gentleman that she was his friend and nothing else.

"Alright Stephanie, you lousy boogie stuck up bitch!" He yelled at her through the phone with anger and hostility in his voice once again. "Fuck you, you fake as bitch, it's cool ma!" He shouted out to her before disconnecting their call.

Stephanie looked at her phone screen and began to bust out laughing to know one in particular once she noticed that he had ended their call. Stephanie had already told herself earlier, that this would be their last phone conversation, so she proceeded to block out his number as she had previously planned.

Stephanie learned a long time ago that The Gentleman held a lack of common sense or education. She threw her cell phone on the opposite side of her bed and began to get comfortable again and watch television; she figured to herself that she was through with unwanted conversation for the evening with annoying men.

CHAPTER ONE

Stephanie was blessed to have the best of everything throughout her entire adult life. She had made it her priority never to forget where she had come from, or to forget about her past. Seeming that Stephanie never had anything in life come to her easy. Stephanie had always either worked hard to get what it was that she had wanted out of life, or she had got fucked over in the end, trying to get it; especially if she took the hustler's route and did a get rich quick scheme to make her money.

Stephanie had tried her best to survive and live her life by the model that she considered and called the right white way. She never allowed herself to engage in any criminal activity, because she learned from self-experience in her past easy come, easy go.

Stephanie was sixteen when she had decided to engage in her first criminal activity. She had gone behind her grandmother's back and had started cutting school and hanging out with the wrong crowd, selling drugs and drinking in the hood. She started cutting class every Friday during her lunch break to go hang out with a group of her friends in Narf Richmond instead of following her grandmother's rules.

Once Stephanie and her friends would cut school, they would catch the bus to go hang out and loiter on Fifth and Market in Narf Richmond.

On Fifth Street, Stephanie and her girls were always able to sell their dope and hang out without any problems from anyone except for the police every now and again. All of the D Boys on Fifth Street had a bad habit of running up on the cars that were potential drug users trying to buy their dope from them.

The D Boys would run up to the vehicles, forcing the user to purchase their dope instead of buying from any of the other pushers that were out hanging on the block with them. No matter what the user said to the dealer about trying to buy dope from someone else, they were always forced into buying their drugs from whoever was the first D Boy that they had come in contact with them.

It was almost summer, and close to the end of the school year for Stephanie and her friends. On this day, in particular, all of the D Boys had been hanging out in front of the corner store on

Fifth Street,   loitering around and pushing their dope without a care in the world as they had always done time and time before.

Stephanie and her girls had cut school early that morning before lunch to join the rest of the crowd and hang out in the hood and baste in the summer sun doing nothing. The girls had decided early in the morning while they were still at school that they were going to leave before lunch and head out to the hood instead of leaving at noon like they usually would.

Stephanie and her friends had decided that they would push the rest of their dope that morning so they could have enough money to spend the upcoming weekend.

Stephanie and her friends met up during the second period as planned to leave school and make their way to the hood. They walked down the street towards the corner of San Pablo Ave and Market Street to catch the seventy-six bus that was headed towards Narf Richmond.

It was busy at school that Friday, so the girls figured they had a good chance of getting away with leaving earlier than planned without being caught by school security. The girls had made enormous plans for themselves that weekend, and they needed to get to the hood quick. They planned on going shopping and taking group pictures so they could post them up in the Market Street corner store that following week.

The girls needed to push off the extra dope that they had so that they could have more than enough money to do everything they had planned to do for that weekend. Once their bus had arrived at their stop, all six of the girls hopped right on, walking straight towards the back.

Once the bus had road pass the corner store on Market, one of Stephanie's friends had eagerly jumped up to pull the bell that signaled the driver that someone had wanted the next stop. The girls could see that the streets were packed that day, and everybody who was anybody was out everywhere hanging. The girls had jumped off of the bus as soon as the driver pulled over for them to exit. Once they had got off, they headed up the street away from the Market Street store towards the back of the alleyway towards the creek to retrieve their dope. Stephanie and her girls had known better than to ever bring any of their drugs with them to school.

The girls kept their dope hidden in the creek in the back bushes, away from the block where everyone else could see. Once they got their dope, they made their way towards the neighborhood where the rest of the D Boys were hanging out on Fifth and Market. Money had been rolling in all that morning like never before; customers were pouring in by the dozen, nonstop and back-to-back until all of a sudden out of nowhere, all of the fast-flowing drug traffic had suddenly stopped.

No one had noticed anything out of the ordinary with the sudden change of drug activity that morning. Everyone had assumed that business was booming as usual. A dope fen had walked up towards the crowd to start entertaining everyone and showing out by acting crazy as if he was a fool. The dope fen had popped up out of nowhere and was trying his best to distract everyone hanging out that day by throwing them off of their game.

Everyone on the block had started to get entertained by the crackhead just as the task force unit was sneaking up on them. The police task force had pulled up in unmarked cars and police vehicles; they even had swat vans with them as well as enough officers to jump out on each individual. No one had seen it coming or ever knew what was happening, and no one had stood a chance.

That year when Stephanie had got herself caught up in the

dope raid on Fifth and Market Street, she had decided then to dedicate her life to success without any crime involved in it at all; instead, she wanted to do things that she considered the right and white way of living.

Stephanie and her mother were never the best of friends, nor had they ever seen eye-to-eye on anything with one another. They didn't share the traditional mother-daughter relationship as it should have been.

Stephanie's mother had given birth to her when she was only sixteen, and Stephanie had been living with her grandmother ever since. Her father, on the other hand, wasn't any better; he was twenty-three years older than her mother, and he never had anything to do with her.

Stephanie had later learned about her parents' age difference when she was fourteen years old and in junior high school. She was snooping around in her grandmother's bedroom through her things one evening after school, claiming that she was looking for something to write about for her history report at school. Stephanie had found newspaper clippings and magazine articles that her grandmother had stored inside of a Ziploc bag in the back of her closet inside of an old shoe box.

Once Stephanie had found out about her father and mothers age difference, she had then decided that it was time to speak with her grandmother about both of her parents. Stephanie's grandmother had never mentioned anything about her parents to her, nor did she have anything to hide from Stephanie about either one of them.   Stephanie's grandmother didn't mind telling her the truth about her parents that night before they had sat down to have dinner. Stephanie's grandmother had explained to her everything that she had wanted to know about the both of them.

After dinner that night, all types of thoughts had raced through Stephanie's head as she thought to herself about her parents; she couldn't believe what she had found out about them. Stephanie had wanted for her grandmother to give her answers about her parents that she couldn't explain to her or give. When her grandmother had filled her in about her parent's age difference, Stephanie had wondered to herself what made her mom want such an older man. She had further gone on to question herself as to why her father had wanted a girl as young as her mother to have his kid; Stephanie had wanted to know why her grandmother had allowed it to even happen in the first place seeming that her daughter was so young and her father was an older man.

A wind had whistled against her grandmother's living room window late that night as Stephanie had sat at her grandmother's house, stewing in her thoughts about her parents. She was sitting in her grandmother's living room on the sofa reading her biology book, studying for a test that she had to take later on in the week.

Stephanie couldn't concentrate on studying for her test that night due to her thoughts drifting in and out of her head about both of her parents. Stephanie had wanted to approach her mother about the situation to get the answers that her grandmother couldn't give her. At one point, Stephanie had decided to herself that she had no longer cared for either one of her parents since her grandmother had been the one who raised her without any of their interference.

Stephanie never spoke with her mother in regards to their situation since it seemed that she never cared for her in the first place. She never knew if her biological father was the man who her mother and grandmother claimed he was since he had never come around. Stephanie had felt that if it weren't for her snooping around in her grandmother's closet and going through her things, she would have never found out anything about either one of her

parents.

Neither one of Stephanie's parents had mattered to her

anymore since her mother left her to be raised by her grandmother

when she was only three months old. Far as Stephanie was

concerned, her mother had given her away so she could start a new

life and be with her husband and their two kids.

Stephanie grew up heartless and cold-blooded; she had

become the type of woman most men were warned about by their

parents. She was her own biggest fan, and there wasn't a man on

this Earth she couldn't have on her team, or to herself.

Stephanie had always been told to dream big and to aim even

higher; she was taught to set goals for herself bigger than average

throughout life. Her grandmother had always informed her that it

was essential to be a leader and never a follower. Stephanie could

still hear her grandmother telling her that there was nothing in this

world that she couldn't have or achieve. Her grandmother told her

about living and enjoying life now, all while preparing for her

future. Stephanie's grandmother would always ask her, "Why do

you want to live average when you have always dreamed of living big?"

Stephanie had stood five feet and eleven inches tall with soft, caramel, cocoa-brown skin. She was no different from any other woman her age. Although Stephanie wasn't picture perfect, she still chose to carry herself to a higher standard.

Stephanie carried herself to receive the utmost respect from any and everyone, and she demanded anyone's attention. Her facial features were the most influential features of her body. She had a natural sex appeal to herself with slanted hazel eyes. Stephanie's eyes could be hypnotizing to any man that looked or stared in her direction.

Not only was Stephanie cocky and self-centered, but she was also overconfident of herself as well. The acne on her face was just one of the flaws that she refused to let stand out. Stephanie had an hourglass shape, with hips that most women would die for; Stephanie was what men considered to be thick. Not only did she have the perfect hourglass figure, but she also had a huge round butt to go along with it.

"Stephanie don't you let that pretty little face of yours get you into any trouble now, you hear me." Stephanie could hear her grandmother yelling at her. Every time Stephanie pranced and danced around in her grandmother's bedroom mirror admiring her self-beauty, her grandmother would come barging in right behind her and shut everything down.

Stephanie loved her grandmother and had always cherished every word that she had said. She could never forget her grandmother speaking to her, "Live life for today, no one is ever promised tomorrow." Her grandmother would drill her to the point where she was only allowed to dream big and to aim and achieve even higher.

"Don't you allow anyone in this world to tell you that you can't do it because you're black or because you're a woman, Stephanie! I want for you to prove everyone wrong, and do whatever it is that you were set out to do, and do what keeps you happy. The only person that can ever hold you back or stop you from achieving your dreams in life, Stephanie, is you."

Stephanie could hear her grandmother preaching to her about the definition and meaning of life as a lesson in the back of her head. Her grandmother had always told her, that one day those words would become her way of living.

Stephanie was her grandmother's youngest and favorite grandchild out of fifteen other grandchildren. Her grandmother put extra interest and care into her well-being due to her not having either one of her parents. Everywhere her grandmother went, she made sure she always had Stephanie close beside her right in tow.

Stephanie grew up to be thankful for everything that her grandmother did for her by providing and caring for her as a child. Stephanie had grown up to appreciate her grandmother's ways; she figured to herself that without her grandmother's upbringing and teachings about life and living, she would be lost with the rest of the world and confused in so many different ways. By her grandmother teaching her self-respect as well as pride and loyalty as a teen, she was able to roam freely and do as she pleased.

Stephanie was mature for her age, and her grandmother was able to trust her with just about anything. Her grandmother had trusted her so much that she allowed Stephanie to do more than most teenagers her age. Her grandmother had so much confidence and faith in Stephanie that she allowed her to start driving her 1997 Buick Regal GS back and forth to school when she was only in the ninth grade. It wasn't until one of the yard supervisors at

Stephanie's school had noticed her driving by herself back and forth to school. The yard supervisor had seen Stephanie because she always had her music blaring through her speakers every single day. The yard supervisor placed a complaint with the school's principal about Stephanie driving herself back and forward to school without a driver's license or learners permit.

The yard supervisor knew Stephanie wasn't old enough to drive back and forth to school every day by herself, so he immediately placed a call to the principal's office to have them notify her guardian and see if they were aware of her driving. The principal contacted Stephanie's grandmother that morning to verify that she was mindful of Stephanie driving back and forth to school without a license or learner permit. Once the principal called her grandmother complaining about her driving to school, her grandmother had no choice but to take her car away.

In late spring, around Mother's day, Stephanie's grandmother had passed away from a mild stroke. Stephanie was about to graduate from high when she had heard of her grandmothers passing. Although Stephanie grandmother had just passed away, Stephanie's mind was at ease, because she knew that her grandmother was at peace.

Stephanie's grandmother had always told her about the definition and meaning of living life with one day having to face the outcome of death. Stephanie had lost the one person in her life who had cared for her the most.

Stephanie never knew much about her father before her grandmother passed away. When she found out about her parents' age difference, her grandmother decided it was time for her to meet her older half-sister, Lisa. Lisa was Stephanie's older sister from their father's side of the family. Once Lisa and Stephanie found out about each other, the two of them had become inseparable. Lisa stayed by Stephanie's side throughout it all; she had welcomed Stephanie into her life with open arms. Lisa didn't have any children of her own to care for, and she didn't have any other siblings outside of Stephanie.

Stephanie's grandmother had always known about Lisa but never took the time out to introduce the two to one another. Once Stephanie started getting herself into trouble and hanging out with the wrong crowd and selling drugs and cutting school, her grandmother decided it was time for her to meet her older half-sister, Lisa.

Stephanie's grandmother had never given her a reason for not introducing the two of them sooner. Stephanie's grandmother had felt that if Stephanie wanted to meet her older sister, then she would have asked her about her the same way she had asked her about her parents when she first found out about them while snooping around through her grandmother's things.

It wasn't until Stephanie was sent to juvenile hall that her grandmother decided it was time for her and her older half-sister to meet. One weekend when her grandmother had come to visit her, she had agreed to bring Lisa along with her to visit Stephanie.

Stephanie's grandmother had decided earlier in the week that she would bring Stephanie's older half-sister along with her to meet Stephanie. Her grandmother had sat the two girls down at the visiting room table and flat out told them both with no explanation, "This here, Stephanie, is you older half-sister, Lisa," while pointing in Lisa's direction.

Stephanie looked at Lisa with a blank stare on her face, and before the two girls were able to speak with one another, her grandmother had interrupted them.

"Stephanie, now this here is your father's daughter, and if anything were to ever happen to me, you would be looked after and cared for by her. Stephanie, I know Lisa will provide for you just as I did," her grandmother had further gone on to tell her. After visiting that day, Stephanie had never questioned her grandmother or Lisa after meeting one another for the first time.

Once Stephanie's grandmother had passed away, Stephanie had moved in with her older sister Lisa immediately after that.

Lisa was full of life on the other hand, and she knew the definition of living it. Lisa was open minded with a warm loving and caring heart, and spirit. Lisa was what people considered to be the real definition of living life to it's fullest, and she had enjoyed every day that she had lived in it.

Stephanie had begun to admired her older sister so much that she wanted to be just like her in so many different ways. Stephanie had felt like Lisa had it all; not only did she have the best men under her belt, but Lisa had also held a decent career as well.

Lisa had owned her own home in the Oakland Skyline Hills, and she was considered to have expensive taste and high maintenance. Not only was Lisa considered high maintenance and upper class, Lisa would only allow herself to be seen driving in the most beautiful foreign cars that were out and in style at that particular time of year. Lisa had lived the good life, and she was the true meaning of living. Lisa had worked hard for everything that she had owned and had; Lisa had felt that if she taught Stephanie the real sense of hard work and dedication, then she too could one day learn to appreciate the value of living.

Lisa had wanted for her younger sister to understand that there was no easy way to cheat life out of what it was that she wanted. Lisa wanted for Stephanie to know that if she took the fast and easy way to get by in life, she would sooner or later lose everything that she had, along with her freedom.

Lisa had taught Stephanie that if she stayed focused and consistent with herself and her dreams, she would have no time for anyone or anything else other than her accomplishments. Lisa Had wanted for Stephanie to no that it was okay to have fun in life now and then, but at the same time, she also wanted for her younger sister to notice that to have fun in life, you had to work hard in the end. Lisa had taught Stephanie to set goals for herself throughout the rest of her life and to never forget about her goals, and always to remember to achieve her dreams.

Lisa was the perfect example of hard work and dedication; she wanted to show Stephanie that hard work eventually paid off in the end. Lisa had known that everything in life was a blessing for her, and she had also understood that it was a blessing for her to be living in it.

Stephanie would always play around, and tee's her older sister by referring to her as being rich; Lisa would still correct Stephanie and referred to herself as being blessed and financially stable.

Lisa was a single woman that had always taken an interest in dating random men; Lisa wasn't into a committed relationship at the time that Stephanie had come to live with her, nor had Lisa been taking anyone seriously at the time. Stephanie was only seventeen when she went to live with Lisa, and Lisa had made sure that Stephanie was her top priority.

Lisa was eight years older than Stephanie when she first moved in, and she had been working for the Mayor's office ever since she'd graduated from high school. Stephanie's grandmother had known that by introducing them to one another, she could trust Lisa to continue raising Stephanie into the woman that she had intended for her to be, and lead her in the right direction.

When Stephanie's grandmother had passed away, her older sister Lisa had immediately stepped in as she had always promised. Lisa knew Stephanie didn't have anyone else to go to except for her, so she had made sure that she had stuck with her word.

The day of Stephanie's grandmother's funeral, Lisa had shown up to Stephanie's grandmother's house to pick her up as promised.

Stephanie was sitting on the patio of her grandmother's back porch after her funeral service; earlier that day alone to herself, looking as if she had lost her best friend. Lisa could remember Stephanie having a look on her face as if she was trying to piece her life back together again and figure out what it was she was going to do first, or which way it was that she was going to turn.

"Hey baby sis," Lisa hat said once she had noticed Stephanie sitting on the back porch alone. "Are you okay, baby?" Lisa had further gone to ask her while taking a seat in the empty chair beside her. "How are things holding up for you since your grandmother's passing, Steph?" Lisa asked while reaching out to hold her younger sister's hand. Stephanie had looked up at her older sister with a face full of tears, silently crying to herself.

Stephanie had begun to wipe away the tears from her face with the sleeve of her shirt once she had noticed that Lisa came to get her.

Lisa looked over towards Stephanie with a massive smile on her face; she had got up from her chair to now embrace her younger sister with a warm, loving hug knowing that she felt better with her being there. Stephanie had stood up from her chair as well to reach back out to her older sister and do the same. Lisa was now hugging Stephanie tight in her arms when she had decided to ask her about her parents.

"Stephanie, have you heard anything from your mother or our father since your grandmother passed away?" Lisa had asked her with a look of concern on her face.

"No, I haven't seen or heard anything from either one of them," Stephanie had gone on to tell her.

Lisa and Stephanie continued to sit on the back porch and talk late into the night, until well after everyone had left. None of Stephanie's other family members had ever come to the back porch to check up on her after the service was over.

Stephanie had filled Lisa in on everything that had been going on since her grandmother passed away; she had told Lisa that her grandmother left her a large lump sum of money and that the rest of the family turned their backs on her for receiving it.

Lisa became upset once Stephanie had filled her in on everything that was going on with her mother's side of the family. She found herself reminding Stephanie that the rest of her family never mattered to her from the beginning anyway.

Lisa had become extremely close to Stephanie after her grandmother passed away; she found herself stressing to Stephanie while coming up under her that her body was her temple and her womanhood was her everything.

"Stephanie, a man will only do to you what you allow him to do throughout your entire life." Lisa had made sure that she told Stephanie to never settle for less than what she was worth when it came to men.

Lisa had stressed for her younger sister to make sure her hustle was always legal and legit. She had warned Stephanie that if she ever tried to cheat life and scam on her riches that the white man, or any other man for that matter, would one day be more than eager to take everything at some point of her life.

Stephanie could often find herself reminiscing about Lisa telling her always to look up and hold her head up high and embrace the opportunity of living.

CHAPTER TWO

"Stephanie where the fuck are you? Girl are you okay? Did that crazy ass fat nigga attack you or something? Bitch say something." Shay had yelled through the phone, once Stephanie had finally decided to answer for her.

Stephanie's cell phone was ringing off the hook repeatedly nonstop back to back earlier that morning. She was unable to answer her phone right away when it had first started ringing the first three times repeatably. Stephanie had overslept by two hours that morning instead of waking up at six am as she had usually done.

Stephanie was in a hurry, and she had no time to answer her cellphone that was still ringing uncontrollably on her bedroom desk. In spite of the fact that she was short on time as a result of oversleeping, she rushed to answer her phone anyway, knowing that it would continue to ring if she did do otherwise.

Stephanie was up late into the night, making sure that all of the paperwork for her new contract was set straight. When she had finally decided to go to bed that night, it was already 3:00 AM and Stephanie knew that three hours of sleep wouldn't be good enough if she didn't get into bed right then.

Stephanie had held her cellular phone between her shoulders and her ear as she headed out of the door to hop into her Bentley GT to head over to her office. She had placed Shay on hold while she switched over to her Bluetooth while getting comfortable in her car. Shay had continued to fill Stephanie in on everything that was going on in the office that morning.

Stephanie began to laugh out loud at the remarks that Shay was making over the phone about some of her coworkers. Stephanie was weaving in and out of morning traffic all while talking to Shay on her Boise speakers over her Bluetooth as she drove toward her downtown Oakland office.

Shay always had something smart to say about any and everything, whether it was an indirect or a direct comment to whomever she was talking about or to at that particular time. Shay would always ask a gang of annoying questions after whatever it was that she might have just sarcastically said towards you or whomever.

Stephanie had already known that Shay was only calling because she hadn't made it to the office as scheduled that morning. It was Shay's job to assure that Stephanie came into the office every morning as she was expected to.

Stephanie had explained to Shay over the phone that she had mistakenly overslept two hours that morning due to her working late on a few contracts late last night.

"Girl is everything going okay down at the office?" Stephanie had asked her.

"Lawrence won't be in today. Other than that, everything is running just smooth," Shay had told her while sitting at her desk picking at her nails.

"Girl you know I'll be right here front and center, patiently waiting for you whenever you get her." Shay had further gone on to tell her before sharing a brief laugh and disconnecting the call.

Stephanie was the CFO of Hair Magic Studios in downtown Oakland. She had started out at Hair Magic Studios as a summer intern during her senior year of high school. Stephanie was so dedicated and passionate about her work that she decided to devote her time as often as it was needed.

Stephanie was able to start her summer intern with Hair Magic Studio when the owner Lawrence, had approached her while she was attending a job fair in the library of her high school.

Lawrence was out scouting local high schools, looking for someone to work with him as his personal assistant. Since Hair Magic Studio was a new company, and money was tight he was in desperate need of someone to help him right away with little to no pay. And for this reason, Lawrence had decided to search for employees at local high schools.

Lawrence spotted Stephanie in the corner of the library doing a role play with herself as if she was doing a live interview. When he had noticed Stephanie aiming for perfection, by role-playing her interviews he had immediately approached her, offering her the opportunity of a full-time internship with Hair Magic Studios with the chance of starting right away.

Stephanie had graduated from high school when she was only two months into her internship. Right after her graduation, Lawrence had offered her the opportunity to assist him with traveling from state to state to help him promote his company. He had then agreed to pay Stephanie $5,000 a month, plus compensate her for all of her travel and hotel expenses. Stephanie jumped on the offer right away soon as she cleared everything up with her older sister, Lisa first.

Hair Magic Studios had become a corporate name due to all of Lawrence's hard work and dedication. He had all types of people from different parts of the world eager for a chance to get a position as one of his corporate chairs.

Lawrence had never considered leaving Stephanie out, for her 20th birthday he and Lisa had both given Stephanie a huge surprise party at Hair Magic Studios' brand new corporate office in downtown Oakland. Lisa had invited all of Stephanie's friends to her surprise party; she even invited the Mayor of the city. It was a huge accomplishment in Stephanie's life seeming that she had been through so much. Lisa was proud of the changes that Stephanie had made in her life as well as the changes that she had made within herself.

Lawrence had come out with a huge surprise and announcement for everyone that had attended the party that day. It was then that Lawrence had announced Stephanie was the new

CFO of Hair Magic Studios. He had decided to surprise her with her new position during her 20th birthday party.   Lawrence loved surprises, and he had felt that this was the best time to surprise Stephanie and tell everyone about the great news. Stephanie was speechless and had become overwhelmed with the story that Lawrence was telling everyone about her.

Stephanie was now the new CFO of Hair Magic Corporate Studios, and she had never attended college, nor did she know what a CFO was or what it was that they had done. All that Stephanie had known was that from that day forward, she owed Lawrence the rest of her life.

Stephanie had started silently crying to herself once she had begun to understand that Lawrence had taken a chance on her with giving her such a tremendous opportunity. Stephanie had told herself that very same day that she would never let Lawrence down for awarding her with the opportunity.

Lisa had decided that it was now her turn to also show Stephanie her appreciation that night by surprising her as well. Lisa had surprised Stephanie with a brand new 2002 BMW 750Li. Stephanie was now incredibly overwhelmed with the gifts and surprises that she had received that night from both Lisa and Lawrence. Stephanie had felt as if she had been in a dream, and that her grandmother was the reason for everything that was blessfully given.

Lisa and Lawrence were both too well aware of Stephanie's upbringing, so they had wanted to both do something for her. They wanted to show their appreciation towards Stephanie for all of her hard work and dedication towards Lawrence and Hair Magic Studios. Lisa and Lawrence both wanted to show Stephanie that hard work did eventually pay off in the end.

When Stephanie had moved in with Lisa, Stephanie had begun to take an interest in hair and beauty. Lisa had then introduced Stephanie to a friend of hers that could get her various job options with the summer youth intern program. From that day forward, and five years after a mimicked interview in the corner of her high school's library, she was now the new CFO of Hair Magic Studios.

Stephanie had the opportunity to work with whomever it was that she might have chosen throughout her corporation. She'd believed in sharing the experience of each one teach one with everybody, and she passed on her knowledge to whoever was wanting the opportunity. If Hair Magic Studios were ever hiring or looking for new candidates, Stephanie would always inform her community first.

Shay had met Stephanie three years ago when she had first started her internship at Hair Magic Studios. Shay was nineteen and was taking up a cosmetology course at Merritt Community College when she had first met Stephanie and began her internship. Stephanie's first impression of Shay was that she was young, fast, and wild. Shay had no idea of where her life was going, nor did she seem to know which way or direction she was headed. Shay was both her mother and father's only child, and they had always been very overprotective.

Shay was the type of girl who would always enroll herself in school every semester just to get the financial aid money. One semester while Shay was enrolling herself into college, to do her yearly financial aid fraud, the school placed an alert on her name, as a result of this she had no other choice but to attend school full time in order to receive her financial aid assistance.

Once Shay had started attending school, the dean of students forced her to do an internship at Hair Magic Studios. The dean of students had advised Shay that if she didn't comply with her course at Hair Magic Studios, she was going to press criminal charges against her for fraud. Since Shay had been scamming the school system for so long, the dean of students had told her that she would have to show proof of work towards her degree in order to receive any more financial aid money.

Hair Magic Studios had such a good reputation around town that their clients were truly dedicated and loyal. Hair Magic Studios would only sale and use their brand of products on all of their customers worldwide. Lawrence had it set up to where Hair Magic Studios would be the only company that leased out their stylists and make-up artists for anyone who was in the entertainment industry or business worldwide. Lawrence made it to where he was the only company able to lease out professionally trained stylists and makeup artists to any of the celebrities at any time.

Stephanie had given Shay the opportunity to work directly with her as her personal assistant. From the very first moment when Stephanie had first interviewed Shay, Stephanie had then taken an interest in Shay and had decided right then and there that she was going to place Shay underneath her wing. Stephanie helped Shay the same way that Lawrence had done with her. Stephanie and Shay had both known that she was giving her an opportunity that no one else was willing to do.

Shay was doing her work at the front receptionist desk when Stephanie had finally decided to make her way in from the parking garage.

"Well damn Steph, it had taken longer for you to walk over here from the parking garage then it had done for you to drive here," Shay had playfully told her. Shay was emailing her children's father while doing some of her work when Stephanie had walked in.

Shay was raised in East Oakland, and she was the true definition of a real hood chick. Although she was hood, Shay was book smart with street intelligence. Shay didn't believe in selling her body, nor did she believe in selling drugs like a lot of other girls had done around her hood.

Before Shay had started working for Stephanie at Hair Magic Studios, she was out committing small white collar crimes just to get by when she genuinely didn't have to.

Both of Shay's parent's had begged her to get a job or go to college and get a degree before she ended up in jail like the rest of her friends and family. Each time her mother noticed her going out of the door to commit fraud, she found herself reminding Shay of the locations where her cousins and friends were being held for their criminal activity. Shay's mother would always rudely tell her that her folks were either in jail or rotting in hell as far as she was concerned.

WHAMMMMM! Stephanie had slammed her hands on Shay's desk to distract her from emailing her children's father. Shay jumped from her desk in a panic as if she was startled by Stephanie's sudden distraction. Shay had figured that it was Lawrence sneaking up on her and catching her off guard while she was emailing her baby daddy during office hours. Stephanie had begun to laugh out loud at Shay's sudden reaction.

"It wasn't like you were doing any damn work anyway," Stephanie had begun to say. Shay had acted as if she was upset with Stephanie for playing around with her and making her think Lawrence caught her slipping while at work.

"Yo black ass scared the shit out of me Stephanie, I thought you where Lawrence sneaking up on me like that bitch," Shay had told her with hostility in her voice.

"My bad bitch, loosen up a bit, I was only kidding," Stephanie had told her while continuing to laugh out loud. Stephanie had already known that Shay was on her computer emailing her baby daddy through Corr Links instead of doing her work.

Shay started emailing her baby's daddy from work the very first day that she had started. As soon as Shay found out that she had access to the company's wifi and computer system, she immediately emailed her baby daddy to let him know right away about everything that was going on at her new job.

Stephanie looked over at Shay's computer and rolled her eyes once she noticed that she had been emailing her baby's daddy. Just as Stephanie was turning to leave Shay's desk and head over to her office, she had looked over her shoulder in Shay's direction and said.

"I sure will be glad as hell when they free your baby daddy so you can stay focused on your fucking work for once."

For the past three years, Shay had worked with Stephanie she would speed through her work every morning to email her baby daddy without any interruptions during her work shift.

Stephanie figured to herself whomever Shay's children's father may have been, he for sure was a very blessed and lucky man to have her by his side. Shay, on the other hand, was wild, crazy, and delusional as far as Stephanie could see. Stephanie could never understand how a woman like Shay dedicated all of her time to a man behind bars. Stephanie could never see herself in Shay's position of taking care of any man behind bars. Stephanie figured to herself that by Shay being loyal to her baby's father, it also showed she could be dedicated and loyal to her work as well.

"Hey Shay," Stephanie had called out to her through the intercom of her office phone. "So were you able to prepare everything in the conference room for our meeting scheduled this afternoon?" Shay was at the front desk doing what she does best, emailing her baby daddy back and forth when Stephanie had decided to buzz in through her intercom. Shay had listened to Stephanie through her intercom as if she had lost her everlasting mind. She leaned over closer towards her phone and had whispered to Stephanie sarcastically.

"Bitch ah duh what the fuck did you think?" They had both

burst out laughing through their office phones before disconnecting their intercoms.

Shay had taken pride in her work, and in anything else Stephanie had her do. Shay had taken her job seriously, and she never wanted to let Stephanie down or make a bad name for herself. Shay had always made sure that all of her paperwork was adequately prepared and on time despite her emailing her babies daddy, as Stephanie had always expected her to do.

"Whelp Shay, are you ready to get this show on the road and show everybody how we do as a team?" Stephanie had buzzed back in and asked her through the intercom.

"Am I!" Shay had eagerly told her. Shay was always ready to show Stephanie everything that she had done in the conference room for their noon meeting, or any other meeting that they may of had.   "Let's show Lawrence how we can count this money and make ourselves a little extra while we're at it." Shay had playfully told Stephanie through her office intercom before leaving her front desk to head down the hall towards the main conference room.

Shay had made sure that she gathered up all of the contract paperwork that Stephanie had needed for their meeting before heading over to conference room. Shay placed everything that she prepared for the meeting on a two-layer pushcart before loading it up and heading over to meet with Stephanie. Shay had wanted to make sure that everything was done right and set up correctly in the conference room before everyone had arrived to the meeting.

"Hey Steph," Shay yelled from the conference room across from where Stephanie was. "Did you call the caterers to assure everything was ready and would be delivered on time for the meeting this afternoon?" "

"No Shay!" Stephanie yelled at her. "That's what in the hell I pay you for," Stephanie had reminded her. Shay smacked her lips at Stephanie's remark and headed down the hall back to her desk to make sure everything was ready and prepared for delivery with the caterers as she had already prearranged.

Stephanie had known that Shay was lazy and half ass doing her work so she could rush back to her desk and continue emailing her baby daddy. Stephanie had known damn well that she paid Shay too damn good to allow her to sit around all damn day and do a whole bunch of nothing. Stephanie shook her head to herself, thinking about Shay's actions.

It made Stephanie sick to her stomach when she watched another woman care for a non-disabled grown man the way Shay had done with her baby daddy.

Stephanie shrugged her shoulders as she crossed the hallway from her office, heading over to the conference room where Shay had everything set up for the meeting. Stephanie looked over at Shay at the front desk and figured to herself that Shay would learn one day soon–hopefully before it got too late. Stephanie felt if she had to hustle and work hard from scratch to get whatever it was that she wanted out of life, then dammit a man could do the same thing too.

Stephanie felt that all men should be able to hustle and work just as hard as she did, if not harder than her. Stephanie could never see herself feeling sad or sorry for any grown ass man who always claimed that some type of criminal system was trying to hold him down or set him up. As far as Stephanie was concerned, if a Mexican man could go out and sell bobblehead dolls and bubbles and all kinds of other different things in order to make their decent legit living, then why in the hell couldn't the black man go out and do the same damn thing?

Once Stephanie reached the conference room, she opened up the double glass doors and was impressed, like always, with what Shay had done for the meeting.

Shay had the conference room tables set up in the middle of the floor in the shape of a letter setting, which would allow Stephanie to give her presentation in the center of the room. Shay placed name tags with everyone's names on the tables accordingly, assigning each person to a specific seat. Shay had informed Stephanie that each seat had been prepared with everything that the investors needed for their meeting.

Shay had the caterers prepare different coffees, juices, muffins, and other snacks as well to last them throughout their meeting. Shay had already known that this was an important meeting for Stephanie.

Their meeting was scheduled to start at noon, and Shay had everything ready and prepared. Shay had known that the meeting was being planned during everyone's lunch and all of the investors would be hungry, so she decided to have the caterers provide them with lunch as well.

The day had gone by slow for Stephanie and Shay; their meeting dragged on throughout the rest of their workday. All of the investors agreed to their new arrangements in their Hair Magic Studio contracts without much debate.

After the meeting had let out and everyone was preparing to leave the office for the night, Stephanie had commended Shay on the wonderful job that she'd done for her with setting everything up for the meeting.

Stephanie had to admit to herself that Shay did have a way of making her investors feel welcome, appreciated, and wanted. One of Stephanie's pet peeves was being stereotyped when it came to her work; she didn't want to be stereotyped by anyone because they where a black-owned company. Stephanie had wanted for Hair Magic Studios to be the first billion-dollar black-owned company.

CHAPTER THREE

"You know what mother fucker you most definitely got me fucked up. Fuck you, you old bitch ass nigga."

Stephanie was driving through the hood, running some last minute errands and doing a little shopping, when she approached a red light on 82nd and Bancroft. Stephanie had barely pulled up to the red light when she heard a bunch of commotion going on directly across from her at the corner store. There was a massive crowd of people gathering around to watch what seemed like two male fools arguing and clowning back and forth with one another in the parking lot of the store.

Stephanie could hear the two men yelling at each other through her car windows. Both of her windows had been rolled up, and her music was playing in the background. Stephanie could still hear the two men yelling at the top of their lungs, going back and forth at each other's throats with nothing but insults.

Since Stephanie was from the hood, she had decided to pull over into the store's parking lot and see exactly what it was that was going on. She turned on her right blinker as she merged into the store's parking lot. Stephanie had driven past the crowd of people, looking around to see if she had known of anyone, in particular, that may have stood out to her in the group of onlookers that were standing around. Once she parked her car, she was able to get out and get a better look at who the two clowns were screaming and yelling at each another.

"What the hell!" Stephanie had yelled out to no one, in particular, standing in the crowd. She had noticed that her gay cousin, Desmond, and one of his many male lovers were in the middle of the group of people that were standing in front of the store's parking lot waiting to see a fight that day.

Desmond was Stephanie's cousin on her father's side of the family; she and Desmond had met each other the first week that she had moved into Lisa's house. Lisa had felt that Desmond would be good company for Stephanie and had decided it was time for the two first cousins to finally met.

One weekend, Lisa made arrangements for Desmond and Stephanie to get acquainted with each other during dinner. Lisa had felt that since Desmond was from the area where Stephanie was now staying and also close to her age, he would be the perfect person to show her around and introduce her to a few people. Lisa invited Desmond along to join her and Stephanie for dinner one night, and with   Desmond being the type of person he was, he quickly accepted Lisa's offer for dinner, never once asking her any questions about anything else. All Desmond had known was that his older cousin lived the good life, and wherever it was, it was for sure going to be someplace good.

Once Stephanie and Desmond finally met and got the chance to know one another a little bit better, they linked up and kept a close connection. Stephanie loved Desmond's outspoken personality and his spontaneous spirit, and Desmond loved her the same way. The two felt as if they'd known each other all of their lives. Desmond grew closer to Stephanie than he was to Lisa because Stephanie had accepted him for who he was and never judged him for his spontaneous ways.

Desmond was upset with his lover earlier that day, and things had begun to get heated minutes before Stephanie had arrived. Desmond had promised his lover that he would give him some gas money if he came and picked him up from one of his play sister's houses that stayed close to the corner store.

Once Desmond's lover had arrived to meet him at the corner store as planned, he had noticed that Desmond didn't have any gas money at all for him. Desmond's lover had begun to get upset and frustrated with him once he had also noticed that Desmond had the nerve to have him come and pick him up near the house of one of Desmond's other former lovers.

All hell had broken loose in front of the store parking lot that day once his lover had begun to put two and two together and had noticed that he had been getting played the whole time.

Desmond's lover became so upset and angry with him for lying and cheating that he quickly pulled his car over into the parking lot without thinking. Desmond's lover had turned off the engine to his car and placed his keys inside of his front jean pants pocket. Once Desmond's lover had secured his car keys and had made sure that they were in a safe place, he had begun to blow up and go off on Desmond in front of everybody that was standing outside in front of the store that day.

Stephanie had made her way through the crowd of people standing around waiting to see a fight that day, trying desperately to get her cousin Desmond's attention. She reached her arm out through the crowd to pull up on Desmond's shoulder to get his attention. It seemed to Stephanie that all the two men were doing was screaming and yelling back and forth at each other. Once someone in the crowd noticed that it was Stephanie who stepped out of the 2014 Bentley Continental GT, everyone had begun to leave and go their separate ways. With everyone leaving the store's parking lot, it had made it easier for Stephanie to get Desmond's attention now.

Desmond had jumped in a frantic scare when Stephanie had yanked up on his shoulders, catching him off guard. His lover noticed everything that was going on and never once said a word to Desmond about anything. Desmond, on the other hand, hadn't seen anything and continued to rant and rave even after his lover had started to calm down.

"Owwwww!" Desmond reached out to grab his heart to act as if he was having a heart attack once Stephanie had yanked on his shoulder.

Desmond had no idea or clue on who could have yanked on him in the crowd of people. Desmond was a character within himself; not only was he flamboyant, but he was also animated.

Desmond was scared half to death that day at the store while he

and his lover were out front in the parking lot arguing and causing

a scene. When he noticed it was Stephanie who yanked him, he

had never been happier in his life to see her come to his rescue.

"What in the hell are you out here doing making a fool of

yourself in front of all of these people?" Stephanie had asked

Desmond as they began to walk away from the small crowd that

was still standing around and head towards where she had parked

her car.

Stephanie walked Desmond over to her car so that she could

try and talk some sense into him. Before Desmond could respond

to anything Stephanie had to say, a high-pitched male voice yelled

out from within the crowd.

"Yea that's what's up, you better get yo mother fucking cousin

Stephanie, if you know what's good for him."

Stephanie looked around Desmond to see who was yelling out

her name. She had noticed that it was one of Desmond's random

lovers screaming for her attention from the opposite side of the

parking lot. Stephanie had almost forgotten that he was the other candidate at the clown festivities that day. Why did I even bother pulling over in the first place, she had thought to herself. Stephanie waved for Desmond's lover to join them on the opposite side of the store.

Desmond's lover made his way through the small thinning crowd stomping mad, with both of his arms folded and switching his hips from side to side. He made his way to the opposite side of the store where Desmond and Stephanie had been standing next to her black on black Bentley GT.

"What in the hell are you two clowns doing up here in front of these folks' store acting like some got damn fools?" Stephanie had asked the both of them. Stephanie had stood by the trunk of her car with both of her hands placed on top of her hips, waiting for either one of them to respond back to her an answer.

Both men turned to look at one another to see who was going to answer her first. Desmond looked at his lover and rolled his eyes while popping his lips.

"You know what Stephanie, it looks like he is eager to talk with you, so I'm going to go inside of the store and allow his trifling ass the opportunity to fill you in!" Desmond had told her while turning to go inside of the store.

"Trifling!" his lover yelled out to him. "You have some nerves fish, oh baby you tried it, okay honey, you trying it today with me." Desmond's lover had yelled out to him while throwing up both of his hand and rolling his eyes.

"Whatever bitch!" Desmond had yelled back to his lover while opening the door to enter the store.

"Anyways Stephanie, as I was saying before your fish kept interrupting a Queen." Desmond's lover had told her while speaking to her with a soft and moderate tone of voice. He was just as animated as Desmond was. He had talked to Stephanie as if he was the victim of a domestically abusive relationship.

"Stephanie where do I start?" Desmond's lover had asked her while placing one of his hands on his forehead to act as if he was about to faint. "Stephanie, all Desmond wants to do is use me and freeload off of me. Okay so look, mind you, Stephanie." Desmond's lover had further stated to her. Stephanie leaned against her car to get comfortable; she knew that his story was about to get exciting and animated.

"Stephanie I was at home minding my own damn business in

my own damn world. Mind you, Stephanie, your cousin Desmond called me begging and crying for me to give him a ride home," Desmond's lover told her.

"That's a lie, Stephanie!" Desmond yelled out of the store door towards her and his lover. Desmond's lover rolled his eyes and shouted back towards Desmond inside of the store.

"I thought you were so busy in there shopping and shit, why you all up in my mother fucking business!" His lover rolled his eyes and continued to talk with Stephanie while Desmond continued to look around in the store and act as if he was shopping.

"Oh my God Stephanie, he is so mother fucking irritating! Now as I was saying once again, this faggot was begging me for a ride, Stephanie." Stephanie had to catch herself from laughing at his remarks; she could never understand how two openly gay men could call each other faggots all day long.

"Ugh huh bitch, I see you out here showing out today, call me out of my name again bitch," Desmond told him while storming back out of the store to confront his lover once again.

Desmond rushed out of the store and ran into his lover's face to confront him on everything he had been saying to Stephanie about him. He ran up trying to swing on his lover, barely missing

him in his face. Stephanie had seen Desmond rushing out of the

store angry trying to attack his lover, but before he could attack

him, Stephanie had pushed him away.

"Owwww I know mother fucking well that you didn't just do

that punk ass shit to me, Stephanie, okay cool, I see what this is!"

Desmond had yelled out at her. "So Stephanie, you mean to tell me

that my own blood first cousin is just going to sit up here and jump

on me?" Desmond was getting upset with Stephanie for stopping

him from punching his lover in the face. Desmond had started

yelling any and everything to his lover in order to get revenge and

make him go into a rage.

"Yep Desmond, she sure is going to help me whoop that ass

bitch!" His lover had yelled back out to him in a high-pitched

voice. Desmond's lover always loved to cause a scene and keep up

some drama, and Desmond still took the bait. Stephanie stood on

the side of her car with both of her arms folded; she turned to look

at Desmond and his lover as she began to roll her eyes at the two

men. She threw her arms up in the air, disgusted with the way they

both were acting that evening. Stephanie had looked over at

Desmond and said.

"Really Desmond, jump you? Boy ain't nobody gotta jump on you to beat your ass, it ain't like you 'bout that life nigga, so stop all of that fronting and acting." Desmond could tell from Stephanie's demeanor that she wasn't playing any games with him, and she meant every word that she was saying, but he didn't give a damn about what Stephanie was saying–after all, he loved drama.

"Well then bravo to you Stephanie–for one, you think you're all that!" Desmond had shouted out to her while waving his hands in the air from side to side, pointing towards her face. "You always take these niggas side over me Stephanie, your own blood cousin. You ain't once ask me to tell you my side of the damn story," he told her while staring in her face with both of his hands placed on his hips, waiting for her response.

"Well Desmond, if you would allow him the chance to speak and finish, then maybe one day you too can tell me your side of the story as well." Stephanie had told him with sarcasm in her voice. Stephanie and Desmond's lover had begun to get tired of Desmond's games that evening.

"Oh, well excuse the hell out of me, honey." Desmond had

said to her while smacking his lips and turning to head back inside

of the store.

"Girl Stephanie, I don't have time for this here type of bullshit

today." His lover had told her while throwing both of his hands in

the air and walking towards his car. "Stephanie, take your crazy ass

cousin home please girl, I don't want his gas money and forget

about smoking up his weed!"

Stephanie began to laugh out loud and chuckle at Desmond's

lovers. She reached out to hug him before Desmond would notice

and came back out of the store to cause another scene. Stephanie

stood in the parking lot and waved goodbye as she watched

Desmond's lover pull off onto the streets.

Desmond was still inside of the store starting shit with the

owners; he hadn't been paying Stephanie or his lover any attention.

Stephanie had looked inside of the store to see what had been

holding Desmond up and taking him so long to come out of the

store. She had then decided to peek her head inside of the doors of

the store to see what it was that Desmond was doing. Stephanie

had noticed that Desmond was inside of the store now arguing with

the Arabs about the price of his things. Stephanie had known that

Desmond was a hot head and that he always had over exaggerated and started shit. Stephanie had known that her cousin was a freeloader, and she knew that he always used his lovers for any and everything.

If his lover had a bottle of alcohol, Desmond would open up his lover's bottle first and post a picture of it on social media as if it was his shit. Stephanie figured she had enough of Desmond's drama for one day as well, and now he had taken his ass inside of the store stirring up more shit with the Arabs. Stephanie decided it was time for her to leave the store that evening as well. With Desmond's lover already gone, Stephanie had run from the store to jump into her car before Desmond had noticed anything and zipped out of the parking lot.

By the time that Desmond had come out of the store to join Stephanie and his lover outside, he noticed that everyone had left him. All he could see was Stephanie's tail lights taking off up the street. Desmond had then twirled around to head back over to his other lover's house since he no longer had a ride. He walked away with both of his arms folded and his head held down, angry with Stephanie for leaving him that evening.

CHAPTER FOUR

"Hello, may I ask who's speaking?" Stephanie asked while speaking softly into her cellphone. Stephanie was in her living room laid on her sofa watching television, she wasn't watching anything in particular on TV nor had she been in the mood to be bothered with that night.

"What's good baby girl," a raspy male voice spoke into the other end of the phone. Ugh, Stephanie thought to herself as she began to recognize the male voice on the other end. That's what the fuck I get for not looking at my caller ID before picking up the damn phone, she thought to herself.

The voice on the other end of the phone was no stranger to Stephanie. She could tell from his tone of voice that it was none other than Ugly Dude. She didn't feel like being bothered with Ugly Dude that night or any other night after that. She pretended to act as if she didn't get any service on her cellphone at all.

Stephanie had begun shouting into her phone as if she couldn't hear him. "Hello, hello!" She yelled into her phone continuously three times, acting as if she couldn't listen to him. Before Ugly

Dude could reply, Stephanie hung up her phone. Uh uh, Stephanie

thought to herself while laying on her sofa, why in the hell did I

ever give my number to that ugly petty ass mother fucker anyway,

that's what I get for being nice in the first place. Stephanie shook

her head, disgusted with her choice of sidemen.

Although Stephanie was home bored and trying to find

something to get into, as usual, Ugly Dude was not the type of

company she was looking for. Stephanie turned the ringer off on

her cell phone since Ugly Dude was unable to get the hint when

she hung up in his face the first time that he had called. His ugly

ass continued to call her back to back after that, assuming there

was indeed something wrong with her cell phone connection.

Stephanie made a note to herself to add him to her call block list as

well, but like always she pushed it off to the side and went off to

bed.

Shay was on the other side of town enjoying her off days,

hanging out with a few of her girls at the corner store on 86th and

Bancroft that night. Her children stayed with their grandmother

most of the time, and this always left her with a lot of free time on her hands. Shay wasn't considered a single parent, although her baby's daddy was incarcerated in federal prison because his mother picked up his slack and cared for his children whenever he couldn't.

Shay told herself if she were ever to have any children, she never wanted to be considered as a statistic and have a million and one different baby daddies like most young women. Shay had made a promise to herself that no matter what, she would only allow one man to father all of her children for the rest of her life.

Shay's baby daddy was from the south of Texas; he and his mother moved to California when he was a sophomore in high school. Shay met had him a few years later during her first year of community college. She met him after school while she was standing at the bus stop one evening, waiting to go home.

Shay and her baby's daddy had a crazy love for one another as well as respect for each other throughout their relationship. Time eventually went past, and Shay had given birth to his only two children by the time she was twenty. Shay and her children's father had ultimately begun to grow apart and become distant from one another after dating for five years. He had always told her that no matter what they were going through, he would forever take care of his children and be their only father.

Shay's baby daddy Rick told her that she could do whatever it was that she wanted to do with her life. All he wanted from her was to allow him or his mother the opportunity to help raise their kids. Rick had vowed to both of his boys that he would be the only man to ever enter their lives as a father figure.

"???It ain't nothing to cut that bitch off???." K Camp played through Shay's cellphone as her ringtone. Shay and a few of her girls began to dance and sing along with her phone's ringtone before she had decided to answer it.

"Shello," Shay had playfully said while answering her phone. "Yo, where the fuck you at?" a male voice had asked her on the other end of the phone. The male on the other end of the phone had sounded as if he was short of breath and breathing heavily.

Shay wasn't familiar with the male voice when she had first answered the call. She rudely asked the caller on the phone.

"Yo who the fuck is this, breathing all hot and bothered and hella hard on my phone and shit." The male voice had begun to get agitated and irritated with Shay's annoying questions.

"Bitch who the fuck do you think it is that you are talking to? Bitch you know who the fuck this is, so stop playing games with me Shay!" The male voice had yelled back through the phone receiver. Shay began to blush and play it cool as she had now recognized the voice on the other end.

"Oh, my bad baby, I knew it was you the whole time I just couldn't hear you among all of these loud mouth bitches that's cackling in the background and shit out here," Shay lied to the man on the other end of the phone. Shay had referred to the man on the other end of the phone as her secret, no one else had known about their relationship except for her homegirl, Cherry.

Cherry had been Shay's best friend since elementary school. Cherry was among the group of women that were hanging out with her at the corner store that night. Cherry yelled out for Shay, trying to get her attention while she was over on the phone.

"Bitch you got me dumb ass fucked up," one of the women in the crowd had yelled out to another while laughing out loud.

Shay was over at the other end of the store cup caking on the phone with her secret, paying Cherry no attention while she had been yelling out her name. Shay was sitting on top of two crates that were stacked up against the corner on the opposite side of the store.

Cherry and the rest of their homegirls were standing on the opposite side of the store closer towards the entrance when she was calling out Shay's name. Cherry had decided that since Shay was ignoring her the entire time she was on the phone with her secret, she would go over to her and see if she could then get her direct attention. Cherry had yelled to Shay as she was approaching her sitting up against the wall at the corner of the store away from everyone else.

"Aye bitch, so I see we acting funny now, bitch who the fuck are you on the phone with that got all of your mother fucking attention?" Cherry had yelled at her, making it to where Shay's secret could hear her through the phone.

Cherry had noticed that Shay still wasn't paying her any attention, and she scooted her crates further away from Cherry's screaming and yelling trying her best to get privacy while she was on the phone. Cherry had known exactly who it was on the phone with Shay once she had scooted her crates away and started shushing her with her hand to be quiet. Cherry knew that it was

Shay's secret, so she had decided to leave her alone and head back to the front of the store to join the rest of their other friends.

Cherry never got the chance to meet Shay's secret man personally. Cherry had only known him from Shay always talking about him all of the time. Cherry knew whomever he was; he still made her best friend smile.

"Fuck you and that bitch ass nigga you on the phone with!" Cherry had yelled out to Shay while giving her the middle finger and walking back towards their friends.

Shay knew Cherry was nosy, and that Cherry only wanted to know who it was that she was talking with on the phone. They both had occasionally joked around with each other whenever one of them was on the phone with one of their male friends, just to be messy with whomever it was.

"Who the fuck was that, Shay?" Her secret had yelled at her through the phone. Before Shay could answer his question, he started going in on her, not knowing that it was her best friend Cherry who was talking shit in the background. "Yo, tell that bitch to shut the fuck up and sit her stupid ass down somewhere before I come slap fire out of that bitch mouth." He had told Shay over the phone. Shay began to laugh at her secret's harsh remark about her best friend, knowing that he wasn't going to do a damn thing. She told him that Cherry was no longer near her to be passing along any messages.

Cherry continued to entertain the crowd of women while Shay cup caked on her phone. Cherry was running her mouth to the group of woman as usual about a whole bunch of nothing, and Cherry loved being the center of attention.

While Cherry continued entertaining the women, a group of gentlemen had pulled up in two separate foreign whips. One of the women had interrupted Cherry as she was the first person to have noticed the men pulling alongside the store's curb that night.

"Talk about a black man getting it, now check that out over there, bitch." One of the women had yelled out to no one in particular.

Some of the women were tired of listing to Cherry's yapping and lying that night, so they were happy to see that some eye candy had finally rolled in. The women had wanted to make sure that Cherry and the rest of the girls had seen what had just rolled up to the store that night.

"I'm hella mad I'm out here posted up looking like this and shit." One of the girls had said in the crowd to no one in particular. "Here I am a real boss ass bitch, out here slipping and shit, looking like this, hanging out in front of the mother fucking liquor store like a bum ass bitch."

The woman began to get upset with herself since her lover, and a few of his homeboys had just pulled up to the store that night. The woman had shaken her head at herself in pity, as she continued to complain out loud to no one in particular about her appearance, hoping that someone would ask her what was going on so that she could floss out her man.

"Here I am in front of this boss ass nigga looking like this." The woman had yelled out again, still with no one paying her any attention.

The woman speaking out in the crowd always thought of herself as better than everyone else, but yet she continued to hang out and loiter with Shay and Cherry whenever she had the chance.

"Aye Shay, Cherry," the woman had yelled out to the both of them without getting a reply from either one. "I'm about to cut Y'all and take my ass home for the night."

Unbeknownst to any of the women in the crowd that night, one of the men was dating the woman that had just left.

The woman at the store was one of those women who lived on Fantasy Island. Although she stayed in the hood, in her mind, she lived in a mansion in the Hampton's. She considered everyone around her beneath her or one of her peasants. The only reason Shay ever dealt with her in the first place, or even let her hang around, was because her grandmother had been close friends with Shay's grandmother.

None of the women had noticed or cared that she had left, everyone's eyes were glued on the group of men that had just pulled up and went inside of the store.

"Where these niggas come from, Shay?" One of the women had yelled out to ask her. Shay was still in the back of the store cup caking on her cell phone, trying to wrap up her call.

"Hold on for a minute baby." Shay had told her secret while placing one hand over the phone to see what it was that her girl was talking about.

Shay's secret was straining his ear on the other end of the phone to hear any and everything extra in her background. Before

Shay had responded to the woman in the crowd, she had first looked over at the two vehicles that had pulled up that night to see who it was that everyone was so juiced about. Shay had noticed that the two cars in the parking lot had belonged to Mali, the boyfriend of the woman who had just left the store, and a few of his boys.

Shay had immediately placed her phone to her ear to tell her secret that she would have to call him back later. Before he could reply back to her, Shay had already hung up her phone and shoved it into her purse.

Shay had then made her way over to the crowd, where the rest of the women were all standing and gazing at the group of men who had now gone inside of the store. Shay had approached the woman who had asked her earlier if she knew any of the men. Shay had shrugged her shoulders to the woman, indicating that she was unaware of who went inside of the store that night since she was over on her phone.

Shay had lied to the women and told them that she tried to see if she could recognize any of the men when they had first pulled up earlier when she was over in the corner on the phone. Shay had told everyone that she would go inside of the store to look around and see if she could find out who the men were that had gone in.

Shay had referred to herself as the Queen of deep East Oakland, and she had assumed that she knew of everyone and everybody who was anybody. Shay had made her way into the store to check out the group of men that had gone inside. She had entered the store and caught a glimpse of one of the men who had come in the store with the rest of his crew. Shay had known off top for sure, that it was Mali and his team of flyboys, who trailed him everywhere that he had gone.

Shay knew Mali from her older cousin, he and Mali were best friends all while growing up. Shay had despised and hated Mali, although he looked at her as his little sister. Shay knew he was a user and a manipulator with womanizing ways.

Shay had stood at the front of the store by the doorway, checking out Mali and his crew and deciding on what it was that she was going to do. She thought about not saying anything to him at all since he hadn't noticed her coming inside of the store in the first place.

Shay headed back out front where everyone had been waiting

around and standing to see what it was that she knew about the men inside of the store that night. Shay figured to herself she wasn't going to tell any of the girls it was Mali and his slider crew. Shay had thought to herself that she wouldn't say anything to any of the women about the woman who had left the store earlier that night, mainly since she was the one who seemed to have been dating Mali in the first place.

Shay figured that Liz, who left earlier, always thought of herself as better than everyone else. Matter of fact, Shay figured to herself that since the bitch Liz thought she was hot shit and all of that, she would make her reap what she had sown. Shay figured that Liz deserved everything she had coming to her plus more.

Shay grew up hating and despising Liz all of their lives. Liz was the daughter of her grandmother's best friend, and she was always looked upon as perfect by her elders. Shay hated the fact that her grandmother would compare her to perfect little Liz.

The only reason that Shay accomplished half of what she'd done throughout her life in the first place was to outdo Liz. Shay was sick and tired of her grandmother always catering to Liz's wants and needs. Shay's grandmother's friend would always go for any and everything Liz did.

Shay joined the rest of her girls standing out front eagerly waiting for her news report about the men inside of the store. Shay stuck to her plan and acted as if she hadn't known anything about any of the men that went inside of the store. She looked around at her crew and shrugged her shoulders as if she knew nothing and no one.

One of the men had finally come out of the store before the rest of the other men did. The gentleman looked over at the group of women that were all waving and flirting with him as they stood close by, acting as if they wanted him to choose. Some of the women were winking and blinking their eyes at him and, flirting while blowing kisses. The gentleman looked at the women with a slight smile on his face as he continued to walk towards his car. He arrogantly stared back at the women and began to wink and flirt back. The gentleman took out his car keys to pop open the door to his 2012 Aston Martin DB9.

Shay knew that the first gentleman to come out of the store was none other than Liz's boo, Mali. She stuck with her plan and played along acting as if she knew nothing about the man that was getting inside of the Aston DB9.

"One of Y'all bitches better get up on him, and jump up on that shit real quick. And the nigga in an Aston too? Oh yeah, I see you bitches be playing with the game out here." Shay had coldly told her girls, enticing them to take the bait and make a move on Liz's man. "See Y'all, if I didn't have my baby daddy and my man, I would have been jumped on that." Shay had told her girls while folding her arms.

Cherry was the first one to take the bait that night and fall into Shay's trap by hooking up with Mali. Out of all the women that were hanging out with her in front of the store that night, Shay knew her best friend Cherry would be one of the first one to jump right in.

Cherry was always out looking to catch a breadwinner as a man, no matter what it was that he might have done to make his money. Cherry had begun to approach Mali as he was sitting inside of his car waiting for the rest of his crew to come out of the store. Cherry leaned her ass up against the door of Mali's Aston as soon as she walked over towards him.

Cherry hadn't known of any other way to get his attention

other than to use her body. Cherry had stood 5'9 with a perfect dark chocolate complexion that ran evenly throughout her body, from head to toe. Not only did Cherry have a banging body with the ideal shape, but she also had a huge round, natural ass that most women were out buying to go with her womanly figure.

Mali quickly glanced over at Shay once he spotted her standing among the group of women that were over in the crowd. He stuck one of his hands out to embrace Cherry's ass, all while looking over in Shay's direction. Mali knew Shay wouldn't say a word to Liz or any of his other bitches for a matter of fact.

Mali was arrogant and didn't take no for an answer. He always figured to himself that since he had the money and the power, he could most definitely have any girl that he wanted as well.

Mali, on the other hand, was also a bit different; he had the money that gave him the power to have the respect. For this reason, Cherry gave him a pass and allowed him to touch and feel on her just as he may have pleased.

Shay turned to look away from Mali and Cherry, to act as if she hadn't seen what was going on with them. Mali and Cherry continued to flirt and fondle with one another until the rest of his crew had made their way outside to join him.

The men had noticed that Mali was macking on Cherry, so they had quickly joined him and began to choose up and flirt with the rest of the girls that were standing outside of the store that night. The men continued to flirt with the women to kill time and wait until Mali had given them the okay to roll out and leave.

Shay made sure that she stayed back and out of the way from the feast of men who seemed to be just as thirsty and eager as the women that were all standing out front that night. As far as Shay figured, if she wanted to have hooked anyone up with Mali, she could have been done so years ago.

CHAPTER FIVE

Stephanie was standing in her closet picking out something to wear when she had decided to herself that it was time to get up, from the long day of lounging around the house and relaxing the night before.

Stephanie's cellphone had begun to ring and play YG's Bitch Who Do You Love. She quickly snatched up her cellphone, answering it on the first ring without looking at her caller ID. Stephanie had begun to smile and switch up her whole mood once she had recognized the voice on the other end of the phone.

"Hey baby girl, what you doing this morning," Mali had asked her in a sexy, soft, seductive, masculine tone.

Stephanie had thought to herself that she needed to give him a better personal ringtone. Stephanie had figured to herself that Mali was the perfect man for her, he had no children of his own, and he also had what she considered to be a legit, lucrative career. The brother was not only paid in full, but he was also FAF (Fine Ass Fuck). Mali Stood every bit of 6'3, and not only was he tall, dark, and handsome, but he also had his very own personal distinguished look that made him stand out above any other man in a crowd. He had perfect all white teeth with the sexiest smile, and deep dimples placed perfectly in the middle of his face.

Mali didn't consider himself to be the flashy type, although he was arrogant, cocky, and rude. He never wore a lot of jewelry, except for his Rolex watches.

Mali only dressed in Belstaff fashion or Alexander McQueen. He only wore Givenchy or Valentino trousers. Mali never settled for less, and he knew what he was worth and felt he deserved to have the best of the best. Stephanie's heart begins to slowly melt as Mali continued to speak to her with his masculine tone of voice.

"So baby, what is it that you've been doing since I've been gone?" He'd politely asked her over the phone. Mali knew how to make Stephanie feel as if she was Queen, and he had a way with words when it came to his leading lady.

"Hey Daddy," Stephanie replied back to her fiancé.

Although Stephanie openly dated a lot of other men throughout her and Mali's relationship, her heart only belonged to him. She and Mali had been dating for ten years straight, and he always vowed to love her and only her until they decided to settle down and have kids.

Mali had told Stephanie that no matter what it was that he might do throughout his life, she would always come first before any other woman. Mali allowed Stephanie to roam and date other men openly and freely as she may have pleased. All Mali wanted from Stephanie in return was for her never to give her heart away to another man or carry his baby.

Stephanie was used to her open relationship with Mali, and they both grew comfortable with their situation-ship.

Stephanie figured with her career and busy work schedule; she wouldn't be able to give all of her time to any other man outside of Mali. She had grown accustomed and used to her and Mali's open relationship, they had both agreed to live their lives openly and freely until they were ready to be committed and settle down as a family fully.

Stephanie and Mali were both successful young black entrepreneurs. They both had extravagant lifestyles and expensive homes within the wealthiest parts of the Bay Area hills. They were never more than a thirty-minute commute away from the neighborhoods where they both were raised. Stephanie and Mali shared keys to each other's homes, and they also shared their security access codes. They understood and respected each other's privacy as well as each others opinion.

Stephanie and Mali continued to cupcake over the phone about everything that was going on in their busy lives. Stephanie proceeded to get dressed and prepare for a fantastic evening that Mali had planned for them two weeks ago. Mali knew how to please and love Stephanie better than any other man could have ever done for her throughout her entire life.

Stephanie had come across a lot of different men throughout her lifetime; however, no one could ever compare to the way her heartfelt for Mali. Stephanie had mentioned to Mali over the phone that she wanted to speak with him at brunch about some things that were very important to their future. Mali agreed that they could talk about whatever it was that she had wanted to discuss with him later on that day.

Mali had reminded Stephanie that she needed to hurry up and finish getting ready so that they wouldn't be late for their brunch reservations. He had told his fiancé that he would have to swing by his office first to check in on some important business that was in need of his personal attention, and after that, he would stop by the house to get her. Stephanie agreed with Mali and told him she loved him before disconnecting the call, as he did the same.

Stephanie began squeezing into her girdle, trying to get prepared, when her cellphone once again started ringing. What the fuck, she thought to herself out loud while jumping into her girdle. "Hello," she yelled into her phone. Like always, she never checked her caller ID to see who was calling her before answering.

"Ow!" a high pitched voice yelled on the other end of the phone. Stephanie could tell from the tone of voice it was her gay cousin, Desmond, on the other end. "Ooh bitch what you got going on later tonight?" Desmond had excitedly asked her on the other end of the phone.

"What?" Stephanie had asked him, irritated that he interrupted her while she was trying to get dressed. "What the hell do you want Desmond?" Stephanie rudely asked him, sounding as if she didn't want to be bothered.

"Ooh okay Stephanie, I see how bitches got attitudes and shit and still feeling some type of way. I mean damn Stephanie, like what the fuck did I do to your mother fucking ass?" Desmond had told her as he began to get theatrical with his conversation towards her.

Stephanie knew Desmond was looking to start some type of drama with her, and right then wasn't the time for it. Before Desmond could get started good with Stephanie; she began to laugh out loud at him before disconnecting the call.

Stephanie had known that Desmond was dramatic, and she knew that he would never let her hear the end of it if she didn't take control and politely hang up her phone. Stephanie knew she would never be able to finish getting ready in time for Mali to meet her with Desmond yapping on the phone about a bunch of nothing.

Stephanie's doorbell began to ring throughout the downstairs foyer in her home. She had already told her housekeeper earlier that it was okay for her to get the door. Stephanie had known that it was Mali coming to escort her onto their date being that no one had ever come by unannounced to visit her at home in the first place. Stephanie's housekeeper called her through the house intercom and informed her that Mr. Perfect had arrived.

Stephanie's housekeeper always referred to Mali as Mr.

Perfect. She'd known both Stephanie and Mali for eleven years, and she worked for the both of them through their entire relationship. She always knew to keep her mouth shut and to mind her own business when it came to the two of them.

Mali entered the foyer of the house once the housekeeper advised the butler it was okay to get the door and let him in.

Mali entered the house and handed Stephanie's housekeeper a brown envelope with $500 inside of it. The housekeeper accepted the envelope as she had always done for the past ten years when he came over to Stephanie's house to visit.

Mali and Stephanie's housekeeper knew that the five hundred dollar tips he had given her was his way of bribing her into keeping her mouth shut, and to continue to mind her own business as she had always done for the past ten years. It was Mali's way of assuring that she never leaked a word out to Stephanie about what he did with his lavish lifestyle while out in the streets.

Stephanie and Mali came back to her house later on that night after having a long day out. They were both heavily intoxicated, so they decided to head over to Stephanie's house, seeming that it was close to Discovery Bay. Once they had made it inside, they both cuddled up in each other's arms on the couch in the main living room by the fireplace falling fast asleep.

They had good intentions of lust and sex with one another on the both of their minds that night before making it home, but with the booze and the ride, it was all just a vision.

Stephanie was awakened at three am by the contentious beeping sound of Mali's cell phone going off nonstop. She first thought to answer his phone, but quickly decided not to, thinking to herself that she would kill him if he were to ever think about touching her cell phone if it kept ringing.

"Baby," Stephanie softly whispered into his ear while shaking both of his shoulders to try and wake him. Mali turned over on his side to hold Stephanie tighter in his arms to ignore his cell phone beeping. He already knew it was one of his random side bitches blowing him up and looking for him.   Whenever Mali was with Stephanie, he turned off his phone and ignored all phone calls. Since he hadn't answered anyone's calls all that day due to him being at home with Stephanie, they wouldn't stop calling him.

Mali lied to Stephanie and told her that it was most likely someone calling about business at one of his sites. Since Mali did lease out contractors for all types of construction companies, Stephanie minded his cellphone no attention.

Mali reached over Stephanie's head to pick up his cellphone that was ringing in his pants pocket and turned off his ringer since he forgot to do so earlier when he first got to her house. Mali grabbed Stephanie closer to him and held her tightly underneath his arms, giving her all of the pleasures and satisfaction they were both lusting for.

CHAPTR SIX

"I can't believe this bitch ass nigga isn't answering his mother fucking phone for me; this nigga got me out here taking all types of criminal risks and chances for his mark ass, while he somewhere laid up with some punk ass bitch." Liz had thought to herself as she continued to blow Mali's phone up.

"This nigga got the nerve not to answer his mother fucking phone for me, the mother fucking dawn diva."

Liz was over the top pissed off with Mali, and she was frustrated with him as well for not answering any of her phone calls. Liz had been blowing up Mali's phone uncontrollably nonstop for the past two days straight. She continued to rant and rave about Mali not answering his phone for her to no one in particular as she sat home alone in a rage.

Liz knew Mali was a street nigga, but she had no idea of what type of dog ass street nigga he really was. The only reason Liz was into Mali was due to his street credibility as well as his financial stability.

Mali made Liz feel as if she was Queen Bitch, and there was no competition for anyone else when it came to her. In Liz's eye's, Mali gave her the world and anything that came with it.

Liz and Mali were dating off and on for the past six months. After their first month of dating, Mali begin to gain trust in her, and with that assurance, he had gained for Liz, he knew how to use her for his white collar team and personal self-gain. Mali figured to himself that he could put Liz on his team and make her one of his main working bitches.

Mali had decided one morning that it was time for him to put Liz up on game and hook her up with his fraud ring. He took the time out to hook up Liz with a few fraud shops of her own for her profit.

Mali told Liz over breakfast one morning everything that she needed to know in order to have self-control of her new lucrative business. Mali had advised Liz that she would be able to gather up whomever it was that she had wanted to work with in her crew. Mali had also stressed to her that no one in her crew should ever know anything about him, or where it was that she got her work from. Liz sat across the kitchen table from Mali that morning, soaking up all of his game. She looked him directly in the face with a straight eye, taking in every single word that he was saying. In Liz's mind, she struck gold by hooking up with Mali, and in Mali's mind, he figured that he had just found the perfect new side bitch.

They had both agreed that Liz would have a team of people ready to head out to work within the next few weeks. From that morning when Mali introduced Liz to his fraud ring, he immediately sent her and her girls out on all type of different fraud adventures and schemes.

When Liz hooked up with Mali, she became cocky and arrogant overnight. Liz figured to herself that she had it made for the rest of her life as long as she correctly behaved for Mali.

The only thing that Liz ever knew about Mali was that he was flashy and paid in full, she never cared to know of him personally or for anything except how could he help her make extra money. All that Liz wanted to do was glorify the price of a handbag or a pair of designer shoes. Liz never once thought to take the time out to ask Mali to teach her about what it was that he had her doing.

If Liz would have known how to educate herself on the type of crimes better that she was out committing for Mali, then she would have known better than to have ever wanted to deal with a man like him from the start.

Liz enjoyed the fact that Mali allowed her and her girls freedom to go anywhere in the country and do whatever it was that she might have pleased. Liz was able to quickly convince her girls to go out of state with her on a few of her runs to work Mali's fraud ring. All that Liz had to do was show her girls a couple of dollars and a few beautiful things, and they were all more than likely to join in on Liz's new get rich quick scheme.

With Liz being flashy and materialistic, her girls wanted in on the hood fame and glory. Not only was Liz able to hop on an airplane with her girls and live it up from state to state, but she was also putting herself on the map for doing the damn thing as well.

Liz traveled for Mali from state to state with other girls that she randomly hand-picked from her hood to work with her in his fraud ring.

Not only did Liz drive a fly new whip on account of Mali, but she also stayed with the latest and fliest labels in designer gear as well. Liz always stayed with a few extra dollars of her own tucked away in her pockets for splurging whenever she felt the need to high side and buy a new Bottega Veneta handbag.

Liz also had the fliest project house in the 65th village of East Oakland to go along with her petty. Liz was what the hood considered to be a real Boss Ass Bitch.

Liz took her reputation and status to the top of her head. When Liz went to work for Mali, he allowed her and her girls to buy any and everything that they wanted with the credit cards as long as they took care of him and his needs first. Mali had set up a small fraudulent credit card shop in one of the spare bedrooms inside of Liz's house. He had everything and anything that he would have needed to duplicate and recreate fraudulent credit cards.

Mali felt that if he led Liz on to believe that she was his leading woman, then one half of his operation would be safely tucked away inside of her home.

Mali demanded $60,000 in cash for each trip that he sent Liz and her girls out on. He allowed Liz and her crew their first test run with Liz being labeled as a Boss Bitch when he sent her out of state with simple instructions to get the money.

On Liz's very first test run, her and her girls opened up and scored high with flying colors. Liz was sending Mali back $60,000

in less than three days of being out on her first trip. Once Mali seen

that Liz was hungry and able to score big, he made her hood rich

and head of his East Oakland female slider crew within the next six

months of them first meeting.

Liz refused to let go of her new fame and fortune that Mali

had given her. Mali went out and coped Liz a brand new 2013

Mercedes Benz CL 500, to show her his appreciation. Mali had

bought the car for Liz to help her better get around in and conduct

his business.

When Mali had bought Liz the car, he never had plans on

putting it in her name. All Liz cared about was that she had the

keys and could come and go as she may have pleased.

Mali couldn't allow Liz to continue running around town

conducting his business all sloppy, by getting rides from any and

every one, he had to make sure that Liz kept his business private.

Liz felt that Mali had given her power, and that power had

made her social media famous. Liz had become the social media

queen and the go-to bitch. If you were ever serious about making

some quick illegal money, Liz was the person you would most

definitely want to talk to.

"What's good Cherry baby?" Mali had said to her over the phone in a masculine, seductive, sexy tone of voice.

"Okay, okay so what's good with you Mali?" Cherry had asked him arrogantly over the phone. "About time you done finally used a bitch's phone number and called me," Cherry had said to him.

Cherry didn't want to seem more thirsty to him than she already did after what she had done at the corner store that night when she had first originally met him, so she had waited for him to call her first instead.

"Aw, here you go baby," Mali told her over the phone, feeling her out with small talk throughout his conversation. "So what you got going on right now, Cherry baby?" he asked her in a more serious tone of voice.

"Shit, I ain't really got nothing up beside waiting for you to call me and put me on with how I'm going to make some of this money." Cherry had eagerly stated to him coldly over the phone. "So what's up Mali, what you got up for us today?" Cherry boldly asked him.

Mali would always go after women that were on a fixed

income, or from the hood. He had already known that turf chicks were still willing and ready to do anything and everything for a label and a few quick dollars. Mali knew all of the women in the hood would be prepared and ready to do anything for him and his slider crew just to get in on his fraud ring.

Mali knew Cherry was a go-getter, looking for anybody to put her on. He had been peeping out her style around the hood for quite some time now, unbeknownst to her or Shay.

Mali wasn't the type of man that would go around asking anyone else questions about the next person, especially when it came to him conducting his business. Although he already had Liz and her crew working for him, he never missed out on the opportunity to make some extra money.

"So do you think you can make some time for me, later on, today so that we can talk and discuss business on how we can get together and both count this money?" Mali asked her.

"Yes, I mean yea, I'm ready as soon as you are." Cherry had stuttered to him over the phone, unprepared for what he offered her. "I mean, I'm really ready right now while you were bullshitting, Mali. How dare you ask me when am I going to have time for you? Mali, you know damn well I've been the one waiting

for you to hit me up for the last two months or so now." Cherry had

said to him before they both burst out laughing over the phone at

Cherry's remarks towards him.

Before Mali and Cherry disconnected their phone

conversation, he told her he would be pulling up to her

grandmother's house to pick her up within a few hours. Cherry

knew in Mali's world a couple of hours really meant later on that

night, and that was CP (colored people) time.

Cherry knew it would take her forever to get herself ready to

go out with Mali. As soon as she hung up her phone with him, she

kicked her heels into high gear and prepared herself to get ready

for later on that night.

Before Cherry could think about what it was that she was

going to wear, she first had to roll herself up a blunt and smoke to

ease her mind on what she was really about to get herself into.

Cherry knew that Mali was the man and that he was always

about his money. She had recognized that Mali put a lot of people

on the map in their hood by helping them get their money. With the

type of track record that Mali had, it was only a matter of time before Cherry had her chance to shine in the hood too.

Cherry was almost dressed and ready when her cellphone had

begun to ring YG's "Bicken Back Being Bool!"

"Yo, you outside already, my nigga?" Cherry had yelled out to

Mali on her phone once she had noticed that it was him calling her

again.

"You know it, Cherry baby, bring yo little short, thick fine ass

on out here." Mali had told her over the phone with the bass from

his sound system booming through their phone lines. Cherry

rushed out of her grandmother's house, telling no one in particular

that she was leaving.

Cherry hated having to stay at her grandmother's house, and

Mali was just the person to help her get out.

"Okay, okay I see you," Cherry stated to him as she walked up

to his cherry fire red 1967 Chevy Camaro SS Clone.

"I see we were riding old school today," Cherry told him while

admiring the car as she opened the door to let herself in. "I like this

Mali." She told him as she continued to compliment his car while

looking around to check out the interior. "This here is fire Mali;

I'm not kidding you." Cherry continued to complement Mali about his car as they pulled off into traffic.

"Why thank you, Cherry baby." Mali said to her with a massive smile on his face, loving the attention Cherry was giving him.

Mali was arrogant, and he loved to fuel off of the simplest compliment. "I see you know a little something about cars out here, Cherry baby." Mali had told her while shifting his gears as he moved in and out of traffic. "What else is it that you know about that you might wish to fill me in on?"

Cherry had looked up at Mali with a glare on her face that showed she was feeling him and every word he was saying. Cherry was joking Mali's style already, and they had been on their first date no more than twenty minutes.

"I don't know too much about nothing, Mali." Cherry had told him while hunching up both of her shoulders as she answered his question. "I mean, I'm eager to learn whatever there is to learn as far as me getting some real money." Cherry said. "It's just that I don't know much about hustling Mali; I really don't know how to hustle at all if you want to keep it really real. The only thing I know how to do is survive Mali." Cherry had told him while looking out of the passenger side window, embarrassed about what she had just said.

Mali had looked over at Cherry with his arrogant, nonchalant attitude before he responded.

"Girl you hustling by doing whatever it is that you do to survive out here and get by in these streets right now, Cherry baby. Look, I'm going to be straight up real with you, I'm about my money baby doll, and I ain't got no time to be playing out here in these streets." Mali had told her as he drove to Hanna Japan's restaurant to take her out for a bite to eat. Mali knew all of the turf girls loved Hanna Japan's Japanese Steak House, so Cherry wasn't going to be treated any differently.

Mali continued to fill Cherry's head with fraud dreams, and turf wishes all throughout their dinner, never once going into specific details with her on what it was that she actually had to do in order to make herself some extra money. By the end of their dinner, Cherry heard enough from Mali, and she was all-in, ready to choose up and join him and the rest of his scheme team.

"First thing I'm going to have to do for you tonight, Cherry baby, is get you a little room somewhere, you know, a little tuck spot off in the cut for yourself," Mali had told her as they were preparing to leave from dinner.

"You know what I'm talking about Cherry baby, now don't you baby girl? I can't have you at your grandma's spot hanging out at the corner store with your girls anymore if you're going to be getting any real money with me." He had told her.

"Cherry, I'm going to go downtown and get you a little hotel suite at the Marriott for a few weeks until I can work on getting you your own spot." Mali continued to fill Cherry in on her new living arrangements since she had proudly chosen to join his team while they were out having dinner. "Cherry, I'm going to need for you to stay at the hotel until I can get you some work of your own and have you properly situated."

Mali drove Cherry downtown to the Marriott hotel while he continued to fill up her head with ambitions of a new wealthy beginning. He'd already known about Cherry's current living arrangements, and he knew that she would be easy prey, Mali had known that once he checked Cherry into the Marriott Hotel, she would enjoy being in a room of her own with privacy.

Mali was like a lion hunting for his prey when it came to

gathering up different women to work for him in his fraud ring. When Mali and his boys pulled up to the corner store that night, he already made plans to pounce on Cherry as his prey.

Mali had noticed Cherry hanging around the hood months before he decided to give her a call. He peeped out her whole style way before she even knew it. Mali knew how to bait a woman in, and that night at the corner store he wheeled Cherry right in.

"I don't mean no disrespect, Cherry baby." Mali had told her as he pulled over into the valet parking lot of the downtown Oakland Marriott hotel. "But uh Cherry, I'm going to need for you to keep all of my business private and to yourself. Cherry, you don't need to be out here catting off in these streets and hanging out with the rest of these broads doing nothing with yourself, and not getting any money baby." Mali had convinced her.

Mali looked Cherry deep in her eyes as he continued to softly speak to her and run game at the same time. Cherry was intimidated by the way Mali was looking at her; Mali looked at Cherry as if looks could kill. Cherry knew from the look on Mali's face that he meant business and that he wasn't playing any games with her. Mali looked at Cherry with a look of death on his face, and it had scared the hell out of her.

Cherry had soaked up every word that Mali was saying to her as if his words were imbibed in gold in the Holy Bible. Mali's words had seemed so right to Cherry that she started counting money in her head and making plans without having done any to make it.

Shay hadn't heard from Cherry in a while since her and a few of their girls last kicked it at the corner store a few months back.

Shay decided to stop by Cherry's grandmother's house to check up on her and see what she'd been up to since she hadn't heard from her in a while. Shay had noticed that every time she had tried to call Cherry and talk to her over the phone, she was always too busy to talk or had other things that she needed to do.

"Hey, Mrs. Green!" Shay had yelled at Cherry's grandmother through her screen gate while banging on the side of her door.

"Who in the hell is it hollering and banging on my got damn gate like they done lost their everlasting minds!" Mrs. Green had yelled back out at Shay through the gate.

"Aw, Mrs. G, why do you gotta be so damn rude and mean all of the time, when you know it's me, Shay." She had told her while pleading for her to open her front gate. "Who else got the guts to come up and knock on your door like this, Mrs. G? Don't do me like that baby, come on now, let me in please." Shay playfully pleaded with her until she decided to get up from the comfort of her La Z Boy to open up her front gate.

"Alright Shay shit, hold on child here I come, you know damn well I'm old and slow while you're over here at my got damn door playing and begging, acting like I ain't about to let your little black ass in here." Mrs. Green had told her while opening up her screen door. "I was gonna leave your little black ass standing right there on the other side of this here cheap ass gate if you wouldn't have said who in the hell you was, banging on my got damn door like that," Mrs. Green had said to her as they began to both laugh out loud.

Shay reached out to hug Mrs. Green as soon as she had come in. Mrs. Green reached back out to Shay to do the same. "What done drug my diva over here to the slums to come and see poor little old me?" Mrs. Green had asked her while offering her a seat on her sofa.

"I haven't seen my girl Cherry in a while Mrs. G, and we

haven't been able to talk on the phone at all lately, so that's why I decided to stop by and see what's been up with my girl." Shay had told Cherry's grandmother while having a seat on her sofa.

Shay peeked around Mrs. Green's small apartment, trying to look inside of Cherry's bedroom while carrying a short conversation.

"Child." Mrs. Green had told her while sitting back in her La Z Boy. "That girl Cherry ain't about to worry me, Shay, she been running around here with some fancy nigga in a bunch of different fancy cars, girl." Mrs. Green had further gone on to say while fanning her hand. "Child I don't know what that woman do with herself anymore." Mrs. Green said.

Mrs. Green told Shay that Cherry moved out of her house months ago, taking the majority of her things with her.

Shay sat on Mrs. Green's sofa trying to figure out how Cherry could afford to move with no job or money. Shay knew all about Cherry's financial situation, and she had also known that Cherry didn't have any money saved up for her to move out with. Mrs. Green broke Shay's silence when she mentioned to her that Cherry paid up all of her back rent and other bills before she moved.

Mrs. Green had told Shay that for the past few weeks, Cherry had been stopping by to bring her money. She went on to explain to Shay that she didn't think Cherry was selling any drugs or anything because she made that loud and clear to her the first time she came by to bring her some money.

Shay couldn't get a word out before Mrs. Green continued filling her in on everything that was going on in Cherry's life. Mrs. Green made it clear to Shay that Cherry told her she wasn't selling her body for any money either, just in case Shay had thought differently.

Cherry lied to her grandmother about what she really was doing to make money. She had told her grandmother that she got a new job with a construction company working in Milpitas. She said to her that it would be easier for her to commute to work if she moved out of her grandmother's house and closer to Milpitas. Cherry had continued to lie to her grandmother by telling her that her new job would be paying for her to relocate closer to their office.

Shay looked at Mrs. Green as if she had lost her ever loving last mind. She didn't want to rain on Mrs. Green's parade, so she hadn't mentioned anything about her suspicion. Shay knew that she would have to get personal and in Cherry's business to find out what in the hell was really going on.

Shay and Mrs. Green continued to chat with each other for a few more hours before Shay had finally decided that it was time for her to leave. She gave Mrs. Green a hug and a few dollars of her own before heading out of the door.

Shay left Mrs. Green's house trying to reach out to Cherry one more time. She didn't answer her phone for Shay as she got her voicemail for the third and final time.

Shay drove in traffic, not paying any attention to the oncoming cars on the opposite side of the street. She was in a daze of her own trying to figure out what in the hell had been going on with her best friend, Cherry.

Shay was at a traffic light with her head in the clouds when she noticed a flashy, bright red Ford F150 pickup truck passing her by. She had seen that the man driving the pickup truck was none other than Mali. She had also noticed that he had a dark-complexioned female on the passenger side of him that day as well.

Shay mumbled to herself that Mali wasn't going to be happy until one day he fucked around and caught AIDS. Shay had always seen Mali in one of his cars with one of his different random or new side bitches every other day.

Shay continued in traffic, thinking hard about the woman in the passenger seat of the truck with Mali. She felt like she had known the woman in the truck with him, her face was too familiar. Shay had known that the woman in the truck with Mali wasn't Liz, who he would usually parade around town with him all of the time. Shay had felt like she dealt with the woman one-on-one sometime before, but she just couldn't put a name to her face.

Shay continued in traffic, heading towards the freeway to make her way back home. She continued to drive while still trying to figure out who was the woman in the passenger seat of Mali's truck.

Shay's mind was on her best friend Cherry, and she would give anything to see her anywhere in the world right that minute. She felt like a piece of her life was missing without her best friend. Cherry had never been gone away from her this long without at least checking in to let her know everything was A-Okay. Usually, when Cherry ran off to leave with one of her random dudes, she would always call Shay first to let her know who it was that she was going with.

Shay approached another red light before reaching the on-ramp to the freeway entrance. Out of nowhere, it dawned on her that the girl in the truck with Mali was none other than Cherry. She had known that the woman in the truck with Mali looked way too familiar for her to forget her face. In fact, the woman in the truck had seemed so familiar to Shay that she came to realize who she finally was. Shay forgot about Cherry hooking up with Mali a few months ago when they were all hanging out in front of the corner store. Shay took out her cellphone and decided to give Cherry another call.

All types of things started running through Shay's head as she dialed Cherry's phone number. She wanted answers from her best friend, and she wanted to know how she could trade on her for a nigga that was only trying to use her.

Shay found herself at home in deep thought, thinking about the safety of her best friend. Her boys stayed away an extra night at their nana's house instead of coming home to be with her. Shay was disappointed in her best friend for keeping secrets away from her. She never thought that Cherry would shut her out of her life for no apparent reason at all.

Shay and Cherry had been best friends for more than eight years. They never kept any secrets from each other, and they had never stayed away from one another for too long of a time. Shay no longer knew what to do with herself anymore without her best friend. She concluded with herself that she no longer had any more real, genuine, down friends or a best friend. She figured to herself that she'd rather spend her free time focusing on her career and family instead of hanging with her so-called girlfriends.

Shay had told herself that day, which she was no longer going to put all of her efforts into any of her friendships anymore. However, she did tell herself that she was going to start traveling the country, living life, exploring, and enjoying different things throughout the world. Shay had figured to herself that from now on, she would no longer keep in contact with anyone who didn't stay in touch with her.

Shay made more than enough money to start living and enjoying life on her own without any of her friends. She figured instead of lending her money out to her friends, who always

promised to pay her back with no intentions of ever doing so, she

should add that money to her savings.

Shay couldn't understand why she wasted all of her time

neglecting her children just to hang out in the hood and be with her

friends. She figured half of the men that she had dealt with in her

life had meant her no good anyway. She went on to notice that if

she ever went out on a date with any of her male friends, no one

ever offered for her children to come along with them. None of her

male friends ever took the time out to ask her how her boys were

doing.

Shay had felt as if she was no better than a prostitute or a

stripper; she felt like they may have openly sold their souls to men

for money, but she, on the other hand, was selling her soul behind

closed doors for the fame and attention of any man.

At the age of twenty-eight, Shay came to realize within herself

that there was more to life than just hanging out and staying loyal

to her hood. She came to realize that her life was about learning

from her mistakes, and it was about taking chances. Shay laughed

to herself when she thought about how hood she could really be.

CHAPTER SEVEN

Two years went by, and Shay stuck to her word and moved her and her boys out of the hood. She disconnected herself from her old friends and some of her old ways and put all of her efforts into her work and kids. She disengaged herself from her best friend Cherry as well.

Shay moved herself and her children further out of the hood towards the suburbs. She had felt that she could get a fresh start on life with her new location. Shay's primary focus was no longer men; she now started concentrating on life itself and living while enjoying it with her kids.

From time to time, a few of Shay's homegirl's would try to reach out to her on social media, but Shay ignored their messages and requests by not responding back to them. Shay's hood had turned their backs on her, and some of her old girlfriends had started talking bad about her and had started assassinating her character for no particular reason. Everyone in Shays old hood had now disowned her because she wanted to do better for herself, and live right.

Shay would still go out to see Mrs. Green from time to time to check up on her, even though she and Cherry were no longer speaking.

Mrs. Green always had a negative thing or two to say about Shay on Cherry's behalf. Shay still ignored her comments in consideration of her being a bitter old lady.

One weekend while Shay was out running errands, she had decided to drive over to East Oakland and check up on Mrs. Green. Mrs. Green had let Shay in as she always did with open arms.

Shay could tell that Cherry had been feeding Mrs. Green's head with all types of negative comments about her. For everything positive that Shay had said to Mrs. Green, she would always throw it back with a curveball and still respond with a low negative blow.

"Yea, so I see why Cherry was saying that you think you are all of that now and little Mrs. high and mighty." Mrs. Green had boldly told her.

Shay had later come to learn from Mrs. Green that Cherry had got herself tangled up with the Feds, in Mali's scheme ring. Mrs. Green had also told Shay that she had just found out about Cherry being incarcerated. Mrs. Green had further gone on to explain with Shay that she had also recently found out a few months ago that Cherry had been committing fraud and hadn't been working at all.

Mrs. Green had told Shay that the fancy dude that Cherry was messing around with was the reason that she had got herself locked up in the first place. Mrs. Green had continued to fill Shay in on everything that had been going on with Cherry and Mali.

It took Mrs. Green two years and damned near a life sentence for her to mention a word to Shay about Cherry at all. Mrs. Green had told Shay that after Cherry had caught her case with the Feds, Mali had left her to hang for dead with no lawyers or any financial support. After all of the money that Cherry had helped him make, he walked out on her with no looking back.

Shay was preparing for work one morning as her boys were getting ready for school. She sat on the edge of her bed thinking about Mali and her best friend, Cherry. She couldn't understand how Cherry allowed Mali to use her and allowed him to get her caught up in his fraud ring.

Shay and Cherry always vowed to one another that if they were ever to hustle and ended up catching a case, that it would never be for a nothing ass nigga that tried to come up on his money off of a bitch. Shay thought it was just like Mali to use a female for his gain, and come upon some quick dough.

Shay had figured to herself that morning that Mrs. Green had begun to grow old and bitter with herself once she had found out about Cherry's federal case and sentencing. Cherry was sentenced to twenty years in a federal prison for identity theft and credit card fraud along with a load of other fraud charges. Cherry's sentence alone had caused Mrs. Green a lot of grief and stress.

Mrs. Green had become so stressed with herself when she had come to realize that she would one day soon have to die alone. Cherry got five years from each state that she had committed fraud in.

Before Cherry had caught her federal case, she had purchased her grandmother a brand new home in the Oakland Skyline hills. Cherry had pampered Mrs. Green with lavish gifts and expensive cars for her to drive around in. When the Feds had finally came after Cherry for Mali, Mrs. Green had lost everything that she had given to her on Cherry's behalf. Mrs. Green had lost her new mink coats, including her new lavish home, and lifestyle.

The Feds had come in and taken everything away from Mrs. Green within the blink of an eye, due to Cherry's source of income. Neither Mrs. Green nor Cherry was able to provide the Feds with any proof to verify their income, nor were they able to give the Feds their original credit card statements to prove that the cards used for their large purchases were in fact in Cherry's name. The Feds had seized everything from Cherry and Mrs. Green.

Mrs. Green had to return back home to her project house, where she had hated living and refused to die in at one point of time in her life. Mrs. Green was just happy and blessed that the Feds didn't send her old ass off to jail with Cherry for receiving stolen property.

Shay had come to learn later that Cherry had told her grandmother to stop speaking with her all at once. Cherry had felt that Shay had run off and turned her back on her for the past two and a half years, for no good reason.

Cherry had figured to herself that Shay, her own best friend out of all of the people in the world, had run off on her and left her for dead. Cherry couldn't come to grips with herself in regards to how her and Shay's so-called friendship had suddenly come to an end.

Cherry had felt that once Shay had noticed that she was finally getting a hold of some real money and a piece of the limelight, everything between them had suddenly changed. Cherry had felt that Shay had started hating on her out of nowhere once she had found out that she had finally hooked up with Mali and his slider crew. Cherry had felt that Shay had run out on her once she was able to bubble up and ball without her.

Cherry thought to herself that instead of Shay being a true and down friend, she had turned out to be a complete hatter. Cherry had told her grandmother to cut off all ties and communications with Shay right away. She had told her grandmother that Shay was only coming around to be nosy and to get into her personal business. Cherry had even told her grandmother that if Shay were any real true best friend, she would have seen to it that she was appointed and hired a paid personal attorney since she had legit bands.

Cherry had figured that since Shay hadn't come to support her during her trial, she was never really a real true friend at all. Cherry had felt that no matter what she and Shay may have been going through, her best friend was supposed to be there to thug it out with her through it all. Cherry couldn't come to understand how Shay had suddenly switched up on her and left her to hang for dead.

Cherry could remember when she and Shay were both young and hung out, selling drugs in the San Francisco's Tenderloin district. Cherry reminisced about how she and Shay would get over on petty pushers and some of the small time hustlers. Cherry could remember a time back when she and Shay had both got themselves caught up by an undercover drug enforcement agent. Cherry had noticed the undercover agent approaching random dope pushers on the corner throughout the night. The agent had later approached the dealers on the block that night acting as if he wanted to buy some of their drugs. After the pusher had made the dope sale to the undercover agent, they were then placed under arrest for possession of narcotic, sales, and drug trafficking. Everyone that the agent had approached that night disappeared into thin air and was hauled off to jail, never coming back to the block.

Cherry had noticed that the undercover agent had decided that it was now time for him to focus his attention on her and Shay that night. Cherry had seen everything that was going on with the drug enforcement agents while she and Shay were out grinding in the TL's.

The drug enforcement agent had then decided that he was going to approach Shay and act as if he was a potential dope buyer. Cherry had took off running without Shay, soon as she had noticed that the agent was coming towards her. Shay hadn't seen anything that was going on since she and Cherry worked on two separate corners.

Cherry had recalled the whole ordeal between the undercover agent that night as if it had just happened. The agent had approached Shay claiming that he had wanted to buy $100.00 worth of crack cocaine from her. Shay had eagerly reached out her right hand towards the agent, to take the hundred dollar bill from his hand him without ever second guessing him.

Cherry had now ran to the opposite side of the street from where Shay was standing when the agent had approached her to make the transaction. Cherry had started screaming and yelling out Shay's name before the agent had approached her, but she was so excited and eager to be out making money of her own that night until she had paid Cherry no attention.

When Shay was out hustling getting her money, she didn't follow any of the rules when it came to observing her surroundings. Shay continued to ignore her best friend Cherry, who was across the street begging and pleading for her attention by yelling out her name and jumping around. Shay had thrown her hood on top of her head and looked back at Cherry all while reaching into the crotch of her pants to hand the undercover agent his dope. Just as Shay was reaching out her hand to pass the dope to the undercover agent, he had then announced to her that she was under arrest for possession of narcotics, sales, and drug trafficking.

As the agent was handcuffing Shay, Cherry had then decided to run across the street and help her best friend, who was trying her best to fight off the agent who was now trying his best to arrest her. Once Cherry had made it towards the agent and Shay, she had tried her best to help by fighting off the undercover agent with her best friend. Both of the girls had kicked, punched, and wrestled with the agent until back up had arrived to help him with now placing them both under arrest.

Cherry had felt from that incident, that Shay had owed her the world since it was her fault that she had been arrested. Cherry had spent three months in a group home due to Shay getting her caught up with the undercover drug ring.

When Cherry was released from the group home facility, she'd returned back to her grandmother's already overcrowded project house without a dime to her name. Shay, on the other hand, had never spent a day in jail since her grandmother was able to sign for her release and pay for her home electronic monitoring device. Shay never mentioned a word about the incident to Cherry again, nor did she ever apologize to her for it.

Cherry had come to realize while sitting in her prison cell that Shay wasn't ever a real true friend in the first place. Cherry had told herself from that moment on that she would never have anything further to do with Shay, far as Cherry could see, she could care less if Shay croaked over and died.

Shay had remained calm once she had found out from a few of her old home girls in the hood what Cherry had been saying about her in the streets. Shay had never mentioned a word about the conversation that she had with the two women about Cherry to Mrs. Green, which reminded Cherry of why she had decided to cut off all ties with everyone in her old hood in the first place.

Shay, on the other hand, had figured to herself that she had never told Cherry to go out and run off with Mali and his get rich quick fraud schemes in the first place. Shay had known that Cherry was out of pocket for even trying to place the blame on her for her and Mali's federal case.

Shit, it wasn't like the bitch was sending me any of her money in the first place, Shay had thought to herself. "Did the bitch forget that she had gone Hollywood on me for no mother fucking reason, and started acting as if she had never known me? So in that case, fuck that bitch!" Shay had ranted on to herself, dissing Cherry while lying in bed thinking about her old best friend.

Shay had attempted to send money and mail to Cherry on several different occasions despite their personal differences. With Cherry being stubborn and bull-headed the way she was, Cherry would always send the money orders and any other mail packages directly back to Shay, refusing to ever accept anything from her.

Shay had felt that Cherry was selfish by not receiving her mail or money orders since her grandmother wasn't able to care for herself and place money on her books at the same time. Shay had known from Cherry's grandmother that Mali hadn't put a damn dime on Cherry's books since she was incarcerated.

"Mom!" a small male voice had yelled out to Shay at the top of his lungs. "Mom we're gonna be late for school if you don't hurry up and finish getting ready." Shay's oldest son had told her from their front living room.

Shay was sitting on the edge of her bed, still in shock from the news that she had heard on Cherry the night before. Shay's son had snapped her out of her daydream and made her put her heels into high gear and begin to get ready for work before she had made him late for school.

Since Shay had moved away from the hood and out towards the suburbs, she now had a thirty-minute commute to get to her office.

Shay and her boys had headed out of their house and towards the car just as her cellphone had begun to ring. Shay had noticed that the number on her caller ID was none other than her boss, Stephanie.

Once Shay and Cherry had discontinued their friendship, Shay and Stephanie had begun to grow closer and became really good friends.

"Hey Steph girl, what's good with you this morning love?" Shay had asked her as she answered her phone across her Boise speakers in her 2014 Audi A8 4.2.

"Hey Shay boo, how was your weekend girlfriend?" Stephanie had asked her while sitting at her office desk filing through a few random papers.

"Girl my weekend wasn't too much of nothing, you know me the same old damn thing." Shay had told her while weaving in and out of traffic, headed towards her boy's school.

"So Stephanie, enough about my weekend, are you prepared and ready for your big day?" Shay had interrupted and asked her, sounding excited about her friend's upcoming wedding.

"Girl." Stephanie had said. "I'm more than ready for this here day to hurry up and come and go already, shit." Stephanie had told her.

"Aw Steph, don't feel that way, it's your big day, maybe you're just getting cold feet at the last minute or something," Shay said, trying to convince her friend that things would get better for her sooner or later.

Stephanie sighed with relief, happy to know that she still had one true real genuine friend that she could always count on in

Shay. Stephanie had sat back in her office chair as she continued to

talk with Shay over the phone as Shay had driven her boys to

school before heading over to work that morning.

"Yes, hunty." Stephanie had playfully told her over the phone.

"It is my day doll, and you are right, I have finally arrived,"

Stephanie said to her.

"Girl, you know that you are crazy as hell, right?" Shay told

her while sharing a brief laugh. "But guess who loves you though,

bitch?" Shay asked her while laughing out loud.

"You do bitch; I know you do." Stephanie had blurted out to

her while continuing to laugh with Shay over the phone.

"No bitch I don't, you tried it." Shay had playfully told her. "That

mystery nigga you about to marry, now he for sure loves you more

than I do boo." Shay had said. Both Stephanie and Shay had burst

out laughing and started to chuckle.

"So Steph." Shay had asked her friend while still weaving in

and out of morning traffic. "When are you going to finally allow

me the chance to meet up with this mystery guy you've been

keeping a secret for way far too long?" Shay had hesitantly asked her. "Girl the anxiety is killing me, I've been dying to know who this prince charming of yours is that got my playa partner so in love like this," Shay told her. Shay remained silent on the other end of the line, waiting for Stephanie to respond back to her about meeting her fiancé.

"Come on now Steph, you know damn well I'm nosy as hell." Shay had continued to tell her. "You've been dating this guy for what ten, eleven, thirteen years now? And I've never once got the opportunity to meet him or see who in the hell he even is for Pete's sake." Shay had stressed to her over her Bluetooth speakers.

Shay hadn't known how long Stephanie was with her fiancé, nor did she care. Shay was just nosy, and all that mattered to Shay was that whoever it was that her boss was marrying had kept her happy.

Shay had figured that she had the power to read any man like a number two pencil. Shay had thought that if she were able to do a thorough background investigation on whomever it was that Stephanie was marrying, she would then be able to save her friend from an aching heart before she had made it to her wedding.

When it had come to Shay investigating any man, she first

would have to check out his shoes, if a brother's shoes weren't right and they were whack or dingy and dirty looking, Shay would immediately have to pass the brother bye. Shay was always judgmental when it came to men, and she would judge any man that had come in her path by his shoes and say, "You can't trust a man who allows his shoes to go up on a Tuesday."

Shay had figured if a brother's shoes and gear were on point, then she would have to go further and check out all thirty-two of his teeth. Shay had always figured to herself that if a brother's teeth looked like dooky breath Belilah, then errt, hold up brother, don't you move no further.

Shay continued to enlighten her boss Stephanie over the phone about why she just had to meet her fiancé. Stephanie could never get the chance to answer any of Shay's questions because Shay had continued to talk over her each and every time that she was about to say something.

"You know I have to make sure you're in the best of care with this here mystery nigga, Stephanie," Shay had told her.

Stephanie had gone into a blank stare as Shay continued to talk to her about meeting Mali. Stephanie had never had a friend that had ever seemed as if they had genuinely and truly cared about her personal decision of men. Stephanie hadn't heard that type of genuine love from a friend towards her since her grandmother had passed away years ago. Stephanie had always reached out to her sister Lisa from time to time, but the bond between her and Shay had been closer than a mother's love for them.

Shay had finally decided to give Stephanie the chance to talk and chime in, but before Stephanie could respond back to Shay, Shay had started to bust out laughing.

"Bitch you play all of your mother fucking life, and you do way too much." Stephanie told her while sharing a laugh.

"Girl I wanna know who in the hell this mystery nigga is, shit, excuse me for being nosy." Shay had told her over the Bluetooth once again.

"Well Shay, if you would have given me a chance to talk before you went zero to one hundred, you would have heard the news I was trying to tell you." Stephanie had told her with excitement in her voice, now grasping Shay's attention.

"I'm glad that you brought that up though Shay, I've been meaning to tell you that I'm planning on having a huge dinner party this weekend so that everyone can finally have the chance of meeting my prince charming." Stephanie had told her while having Shay's undivided attention when mentioning the words, meet my prince charming. Stephanie had gone on to explain to Shay further that she wasn't the only one who hadn't yet met her man.

Stephanie had explained to Shay that she hadn't allowed anyone in her family to meet her fiancé due to their open relationship. She had told Shay for that reason; they had both agreed to keep their personal relationship and lives private. Stephanie had further gone to let Shay no that by them keeping their relationship private from others; it had kept out a lot of stress and unnecessary bullshit with unwanted drama.

When Stephanie went into detail with Shay about her open relationship with her fiancé, Shay's jaws began to drop, and her mouth flew wide open as Stephanie filled her in.

"Mom, pay attention to what you're doing and stop gossiping so much already." Her older son had told her, tired of listening to his mom and Stephanie gossip on his way to school that morning.

Shay's son had looked over at her from the passenger seat of their car and placed both of his hands over his ears and said, "Mom you passed up our school two blocks ago for the second time this morning."

"Yea mom, you need to pay better attention to what it is that you're doing like you always tell us to do." Shay's younger son had chimed in, taking defense with his older brother.

"Mom, you should be a news reporter, you always stay with somebody else tea in your cup." Her older son had said to her as they began to laugh out loud at their mother.

Shay had pulled over to the front of the boy's school to let them out of the car to start their day. Her older son had turned to look at his mom while he was getting out of the car and began to shake his little head at her and laugh.

"Bye Mom, have a blessed day!" Both of the boys had yelled out as they jumped out of the car to head inside of the school.

"Bye babies, Y'all have a blessed day as well!" Shay had yelled back to them.

"We will mom and don't make me have to beat anyone up behind your mouth today." Her older son had turned to tell her while waving goodbye.

Shay and Stephanie had begun to laugh as Shay pulled from in front of her boy's school, and back into traffic.

"Girl, them boys of yours is a fool, especially that older one."
Stephanie had told her as they continued to gossip on Shay's way
into work.

"You know you took me for a loop with that open relationship
shit you were telling me about earlier, Steph." Shay had said.
"Bitch I passed up the boys school two times fucking around with
you and your tomfoolery bullshit." Shay had said.

Shay had let Stephanie know that she was almost to the office
and that she would be pulling up in a minute.

"Keep that teapot brewing for me Stephanie, I'm coming
straight to the office to come and talk directly with you live and in
person." Shay had told her before disconnecting the Bluetooth on
her phone.

Shay pulled into the parking garage of their office, damn near
breaking her neck trying to get out of her car and rushing to
Stephanie to get the rest of her business.

Shay had come into the office that morning giving out fake
hello's and false high's, all while rushing past everyone in the front
just to get to her boss's desk so that they could finish up their

morning tea session. The only thing that was important to Shay that morning was Stephanie filling her in about her fiancé.

"Knock, Knock girl let me in." Shay had announced while letting herself into Stephanie's office. Stephanie was on the phone wrapping up a conversation with one of her clients when Shay had finally walked in. Stephanie had placed one of her fingers in front of her mouth, giving Shay the signal to keep quiet and to come in and have a seat. Shay had sat on Stephanie's sofa and got comfortable facing directly towards Stephanie at her desk while she continued to wrap things up with her client over the phone.

Stephanie had asked for Shay to close her office door once she had hung up her phone.

"Yo ass so damn nosy Shay, that it's a got damn shame, your crazy ass done ran up in here looking for the scoop so damn hard that you left my damn door wide open." Stephanie had told her. "Bad enough I got your crazy ass all up in my business, I don't need the rest of these nosy mother fuckers all up in it as well." Stephanie said.

Shay and Stephanie began to laugh out loud as they would always do when in the company of each other. "Well, any ways bitch." Stephanie had said as she sat up on top of her office desk directly across from Shay on the sofa.

"I just wasn't ready to settle down at the time that my fiancé and I had first started dating, so we both agreed to have an open relationship with certain stipulations that all." Stephanie had told her, feeling her in on the situation-ship of her open relationship.

Shay sat on Stephanie's sofa in her office with her mouth wide open, soaking up every bit of information that she was hearing. Shay was all ears when it came to Stephanie sharing her personal business. Shay was more excited about finally getting a chance to put a name to the face of Stephanie's fiancé more than anything.

"So Shay, are you going to Dubai with me to celebrate my bridal shower in a few months or not?" Stephanie had surprisingly asked her.

One thing about Stephanie was that she knew how to live life, and she knew all about living in it.

"Dubai?" Shay had asked, repeating the question as if she didn't understand the first time. "Why not Vegas or Hawaii or somewhere like that?" Shay asked her, feeling a little unsure about traveling overseas for the first time.

"Girl please," Stephanie had told her while waving her hand at Shay as she got up from her desk to go over to her office refrigerator to get herself something to drink.

"Shay," Stephanie said to her friend with a sigh under her breath. "You need to get out more often; you're so local and boring that it's pathetic." Stephanie had said to her. "Shay, what's the point of living life if we're not going to do anything with it." Stephanie had said. "Look, Shay," Stephanie said while taking a sip of her bottled water. "You only get to live once in this lifetime, and there ain't no second chances, and there damn sure ain't no coming back, so with that being said bitch you better start making your mark in this world and start living in it." Stephanie had told her.

"Shay, don't you dare give me no bullshit about you can't afford it either, I pay you too damn good." Stephanie had further gone on to tell her. "If you stop putting all of your money on that nigga's books then you would be able to live and enjoy the finer things in life. Shay, I'm going to start taking money out of your paycheck every pay period to start paying for your trip to Dubai, this way I know you won't back out on me at the last minute. So do we have ourselves a deal, Mrs. Shay?" Stephanie asked her

friend while holding out her hand towards Shay to shake upon their

new deal.

"Now Shay, you got your passport already right?" Stephanie

had asked her with authority in her voice.

"Yes mother, damn, I got it but it sure in the hell ain't got no

damn stamps on it yet." Shay had told her while sucking on her

teeth with both of her arms now folded.

"Well, that's what's up Shay, at least it's a start, and I'm going

to be the one to take credit for helping you get your first

international stamp" Stephanie had told her.

CHAPTER EIGHT

"Shay girl is that you?" a female voice had yelled out to her from the second floor of the Hilltop Mall.

Shay turned around to look up above her and see who it was that was yelling out her name throughout the mall while she was out shopping that afternoon. Shay had noticed that it was her grandmother's best friend's granddaughter Liz, who was calling out her name.

"Oh hey girl, how have you been?" Shay had asked her, not excited to see her at all, once they meet up. Shay didn't have the same enthusiasm as Liz did once she had noticed who it was calling her name from the second floor. "How have you been girl, long time no see." Shay had told her with a fake smile and wave.

"Like wise girl, and how about yourself?" Liz had asked her with a look of deceit on her face.

Liz was ecstatic she bumped into Shay at the mall that afternoon. With Shay being away from the hood and out of sight for far too long, Liz had decided that it was time to fill her in.

Liz figured to herself that since Shay was close to Mali through her cousin, she would be able to use her to send Mali a subliminal message.

Unbeknownst to Shay, Mali cut off all contact with Liz and the rest of his side bitches. When he decided it was time for him and Stephanie to tie the knot and settle down. Mali had cut every single one of his other bitches entirely off.

Mali had vanished and disappeared on all of his other women in the hood, and it was driving Liz crazy. Not only did Liz physically miss Mali after being attached to him for so long, but she had also missed the money that she had made with him as well. Without Mali and his fraud ring, Liz was flat out broke and unable to stunt and keep up her flashy lifestyle.

Mali had left Liz with nothing but high hopes and dreams. Liz had figured to herself since she still held on to the Mercedes Benz that he had bought for her, he would one day come back and be with her.

"So how have you and your boys been, Shay?" Liz had asked her, trying to engage in small talk while thinking of a way to sneak in a comment about Mali.

Shay, on the other hand, had nothing she wanted to say to Liz or talk about with her. All Shay was trying to do was say hi and bye since she had a lot of shopping left that she needed to do for her trip to Dubai.

Shay never cared for Liz, and she wasn't in the mood to pretend like she did. Shay didn't want to have a conversation with Liz, nor was she enthused with having to continue to speak with her.

"They're just fine girl, thank you for asking." Shay had blurted out to her while fanning her hand out, giving her the signal that she was uninterested and had to leave.

"Shay before you go I wanted to let you know that I was expecting my first baby real soon." Liz had told her. Shay turned around to look at Liz as if she'd lost her everlasting mind. Shay hadn't noticed any bulge in Liz's belly, so she was unsure of why Liz informed her about being pregnant.

"Yes girl," Liz had further gone on to lie and tell her. "I thought your grandmother would have told you by now that I was expecting my first baby, I sent her your baby shower invitation in the mail a few weeks ago since no one had no idea of where you'd moved to." Liz had said.

"No Liz, my grandmother hadn't told me anything about you having a baby with anyone." Shay had told her. Shay had suddenly lost track of what it was that she was doing fooling around with Liz and her petty gossiping.

"Girl I thought you knew that Mali and I are having our first baby." Liz had told her. "Girl you can for sure tell you haven't been hanging around in the hood lately, that's all these bitches been running around here talking about."

Liz had gone deeper into her lie, giving Shay over exaggerated detail about her and Mali's pretend maybe baby.

"Mali's having a baby with this bitch Liz is all that rolls off of these bitches tongues out here in these town streets." Liz had told her before laughing out loud as she continued to juice Shay up with news about her and Mali's pretend baby.

Liz had already known that Shay had a big mouth and would run off and tell everybody and anybody who was willing to listen. Liz had figured that once word had got back to Shay's cousin, who would then tell Mali it would bring him back home to her, and she knew for sure he would come running.

"Mali?" Shay blurted out in shock from the news.

"Yes, bitch Mali!" Liz went on to proudly say to her. "Mr. Money Man himself girl, that's my baby's daddy," Liz had told her, making sure that she had gone out of her way to fill Shay in on any extra's about her being pregnant with Mali's baby. Liz wanted to make sure that Shay and her big mouth had an earful to take back to Cherry. Liz didn't wish to leave out any detail for Shay to tell her best friend.

Shay was speechless after she ran into Liz at the mall that afternoon. Unbeknownst to Liz, Shay and Cherry weren't even friends any longer. Shay just couldn't believe that out of all of the bitches that Mali had fucked with in the hood, he would go out and get bougie ass Liz pregnant with his first baby.

All types of things had started running through Shay's head about Mali and Liz. Since Shay distanced herself from the hood, she didn't have anyone to gossip with.

"Did you finish up most of your shopping yet boo?" Stephanie had asked Shay over the phone one evening while preparing for her engagement dinner later on that night.

"Yes girl, I went out to the mall a couple of weeks ago and got everything done then, after all of this running around I'm going to be way over due for this here little foreign vacation," Shay had said to her. Stephanie and Shay shared a brief laugh before Stephanie had decided to cut her off and remind her about the dinner that she had scheduled for everyone to meet her fiancé later on that night.

"Girl I almost forgot, we are all going to get a chance to meet your prince charming finally." Shay said to her. "So bitch what time does dinner start?" Shay had asked her new best friend, Stephanie, excited to finally meet her man. Stephanie had begun to laugh out loud at Shay, knowing that her best friend was extremely nosy.

"Dinner starts tonight at eight, Shay." Stephanie had told her while giving her housekeeper orders on setting the dinner table.

"Okay well Stephanie bitch, I'm going to call you back, later on, tonight when I'm on my way, it's already five thirty meaning I only have two and a half hours left to get ready." Shay had said to her before disconnecting the call.

It was only seven thirty and Shay was the first to arrive at Stephanie's house. She had parked her car in the front foyer of

Stephanie's circular driveway as told by her valet services. Once Shay had parked her car, she was then escorted over to Stephanie's front door where she was advised to ring the doorbell so that someone could greet her and let her in.

Before Shay rang the doorbell, she decided to take a step back and enjoy the beautiful scenery of Stephanie's lovely and extravagant home.

"Okay now bitch, this is what you call good living." Shay had said to herself before ringing the doorbell to announce that she had arrived.

When Shay rang the front doorbell, she was greeted by Stephanie's butler, who escorted her to the main entrance to be waited on by the housekeeper and maid. Shay was then accompanied into the waiting area by one of Stephanie's housekeepers, who also offered her a glass of champagne while she waited for the rest of the guests to arrive.

"Ma'am is there anything else that I could do for you until the rest of our guests arrive this evening?" Stephanie's housekeeper had asked her while offering her a seat on the ottoman in the front waiting room. "No thank you ma'am, but thank you for asking anyway." Shay had told her before sitting down.

"Bitch you got her hella early." Stephanie had called out to her through her home intercom, scaring the hell out of Shay.

"What the fuck!" Shay had yelled out, almost spilling her champagne on her white satin dress.

Shay tipped her champagne flute up to take a sip of her drink as she looked around the room suspiciously, looking for Stephanie.

"Okay now bitch I can hear you, but I don't see you where the fuck is you at, come on now Stephanie with all of this new age technology bullshit." Shay had said while suspiciously looking around the room. "Bitch you like to have scared the shit out of me, where in the fuck are you? I'm too damn grown to be playing hide and seek Stephanie." Shay had said while taking another sip of her champagne. Stephanie laughed across the intercom at what Shay was saying; she had told her that she was calling from within the house on her intercom in her master bedroom. "I'll be down to meet you in just a minute when the rest of the guests get here to introduce you all to my fiancé.

Shay continued to enjoy her drink and look around at some of the art pieces that were hanging on Stephanie's waiting room area walls.

"Ma'am," Stephanie's housekeeper had called out to her, catching her off of guard. "Sorry to startle you, but the rest of our guests have arrived, and everyone is being escorted into the main dining room, would you care to join me please?" The housekeeper had asked her while extending her hand out to escort her to the dining room area.

"Why thank you, ma'am, I would love to join you for dinner," Shay had told the housekeeper as she was escorted out of the waiting area to the main dining room.

"Let me ask you a question, why was I the only one escorted from the waiting room to the main dining room without the rest of the guests?" Shay had asked her. The housekeeper turned to look at Shay and said. "You were the very first one to arrive, miss, everyone else has just got here, and it's eight twenty-three." Shay rolled her eyes at the housekeeper's response and continued following her to the dining area.

Shay was seated next to Desmond and Lisa, Stephanie's gay cousin and her older sister. The three got along just fine at the dinner table as they engaged in small talk with one another, dissing

Stephanie's other friends.

"Owe, do either one of y'all no any of them thangs over there?" Desmond had asked Lisa and Shay while pointing at Stephanie's other friends who were sitting directly across from them at the opposite side of the table.

"Fuck no, I don't know none of those bougie bitches." Shay had eagerly chimed in while starting to bust out laughing, and looking at one of the girls directly in her face.

"Come on now you two stop, lawd I don't know why in the hell they done sat Y'all two crazy asses next to me." Lisa said to Desmond and Shay while spanking both of their hands as if they were two small kids.

Stephanie's butler had come out to the main dining room, where everyone had gathered around at the table enjoying their dinner. He had announced that Stephanie and her fiancé would be out shortly to join them soon during their dessert course after their meal.

Shay looked over at Desmond and Lisa and whispered to both of them. "What in the hell type of fancy shit is this Stephanie got going on? I mean damn, the bitch acting like she about to introduce us to Bill Gates or some mother fucking body." Shay had said while taking a bite of her veal cutlet, and chewing on her meat like she had never eaten before. Desmond and Lisa looked over at Shay as if she lost her everlasting mind and burst out laughing.

"Shay you ain't got no mother fucking sense bitch." Lisa had playfully told her while taking a sip of her wine. "I don't know what the fuck Stephanie's crazy ass got going on, but all I do know is this nigga better be some mother fucking good with all of this here bullshit she is pulling." Lisa had told Desmond and Shay.

"Well, I know whoever the nigga is, she sure has been hiding him from the family for what, ten or fifteen years now?" Desmond had turned to ask Lisa while sipping on his glass of red wine.

"Thank you all for coming out tonight and joining me for dinner to meet my fiancé, I'm pleased to have all of my close friends and family here with me to finally meet him."

"Mali baby, come on out here so that everyone can finally get the chance to meet you and say hello." Stephanie had told her soon to be husband as he entered the main dining room.

Shay and Desmond looked up from their dinner plates with both of their mouths hung wide open.

"Shut the fuck up," Desmond whispered over to Shay once he had noticed who Stephanie's fiancé was. Shay had looked up and began to choke on a piece of her veal cutlet as Lisa acted as if she was giving her the Heimlich Maneuver.

Stephanie had turned to look at Desmond, Lisa, and Shay as if they had all lost their everlasting minds. She had then turned to Mali and grabbed him by his hand to escort him over towards their side of the table to formally introduce him to them.

"Baby these clowns are my family, this here baby is my older sister Lisa, and this is my older cousin Desmond, and my best friend, Shay." Stephanie had told him while holding his hand and pointing out to him each individual.

Mali turned to wave at them as if he had never met any of them before. Shay, Desmond, and Lisa all waved back and did the same.

Although Stephanie had taken the time out to formally introduce everyone to Mali, Desmond insisted on taking the time out to reintroduce himself.

"Hello sir how are you, my name is Desmond and I'm Stephanie's favorite cousin." Desmond had told him with sarcasm in his voice while extending his hand to greet him again.

After dinner that week, Shay was focused on Stephanie and Mali's future, seeing as Liz wanted them to be unhappy.

Shay had never known while Mali was out hustling and messing around with Liz and Cherry, that he was dedicated and engaged to Stephanie the whole time.

Here it was two months before her girl's big day, and this dainty bitch Liz came pulling up on her with some foul, messy shit like that. Shay had sat at home that night trying her best to figure out with herself if and how she should tell Stephanie the truth about her prince charming.

Shay regretted running into Liz at the Hilltop Mall a few weeks back. She didn't know if she had wanted to tell Stephanie about what she heard from Liz that day at the mall, or if she just wanted to go kill Mali her got damn self and go whoop Liz's ass.

Shay wondered to herself why hadn't her grandmother said anything to her about her friend's granddaughter's pregnancy in the first place, seeing as she spoke with her grandmother on the phone all of the time. Shay shrugged it off, figuring that her grandmother didn't mention it to her knowing how she didn't really care for Liz.

Here it was two months before her homegirl's big wedding day and less than one week before they were due to head out to Dubai to begin her and Mali's life celebration.

Shay felt like a women scorned, a true friend that had betrayed the truth and her best friends trust. Shay had wanted to tell Stephanie every single word that she had heard from Liz earlier that week in the mall, but then again, she didn't want to seem as if she was a single, lonely, bitter, hating ass friend.

Shay reminded herself how Stephanie explained to her about her and Mali's rules as far as their open relationship. She felt like she was in the most jacked up situation any woman could be in as far as gaining a friend's trust. Although her loyalty was with Stephanie no doubt or questions asked about it, she was still raised up under her cousin and Mali, whom she considered brothers.

Shay sat on her living room couch and began to ask herself, "Do I let my friend move further with her life, and never mention to her how I know about her husband's lying and deceiving conniving dog ass ways?"

Shay had figured that this was some tea that she had wished that she didn't have to pour for her best friend.

"I got it." Shay had yelled out to herself with excitement. "I'm just going to go to the hood myself and see Mali. I'm going to act as if I'm checking up on Mrs. G, and I know for sure that I'm going to run into him." Shay had told herself while scheming up on a way to meet up with Mali.

Three days before Shay and Stephanie's trip to Dubai, Shay had finally decided that it was time for her to make her way to the hood and see Mali. Before Shay had arrived at Mrs. Green's house that Tuesday afternoon, she had first decided to hit up every street and scene there was in her hood. Shay was driving up the street to go past the gas station where Mali and his boys were known to hang out at. Just as Shay was about to turn and drive away from Mali's spot and head out towards Mrs. Green's house, she spotted him with his boys straight ahead of her on the opposite side of the gas station.

Mali's boys were squeezing up on a few of the shorties that had come through the gas station's parking lot that day. The owners of the gas station had never complained about Mali and his crew hanging out in front of their store because they had always brought in extra business for him. The owner had known that once

Mali and his boys had pulled up to loiter in front of his gas station, more customers would come just to be seen by Mali. The owners of the gas station had known that Mali and his boys didn't sell any drugs, and they had also known that Mali and his crew weren't the violent types.

The owners had always figured that Mali and his boys were a bunch of pretty spoiled young rich kids, that wanted a cool and safe place to hang out at and show off their fly, flashy, expensive foreign whips. Mali and his crew stunted so hard every day at the owner's gas station that they had intimidated him into also going out and buying himself a brand new 2014 Ferrari 458 Italia. Mali had that type of effect on people in his hood everyone had looked up to him as their king.

Shay pulled had up to the side of the store where she had spotted Mali and his boys. She had noticed that they were hanging in the back of the gas station by Mill's Hoagie shop. Shay had pulled her car into the back where everyone was hanging out at.

Before she had got out of her car to approach Mali, she had begun to have mixed emotions about the way that she had wanted to approach him concerning Liz's situation with him. Shay had thought about jumping out of her car and going ballistic on Mali in front of his boys but had shrugged it off for the sake of Stephanie and for the sake of her keeping her job.

Shay had calmly parked her car two stalls away from where Mali and his boys were standing and began to step out of her car and calming herself down. She had got upset with herself for all of the dog ass things that she had known personally about Mali. Shay had calmed herself by explaining to herself that there were always two sides to every story.

"Yo yo yo, baby banging over there in the ride." One of Mali's friends had yelled out to her. Shay was pissed off that his big mouth ass had spotted her out and fronted her off to the rest of his boys. Shay had called herself sneaking up on Mali and unexpectedly surprising him that day with her pop up visit. But as usual, there was always an old thirsty ass nigga in every crew scoping out every chick that had came through the parking lot that day to see if he could see what her mouth do. His big mouth ass had gathered everyone's attention before Shay could.

"Well damn thank you for the unwanted introduction, king Boosie." Shay had told the man in Mali's crew while rolling her eyes.

"Yo Mali, what's good bruh?" Shay had flamboyantly yelled out to him, demanding his attention while stepping outside of her car.

"Shit what's good sis, come check it out for a minute." Mali had told her while waving his hand for her to come in his direction.

"Aw shit sis, a nigga must be in some deep shit for you to have to come way out here to holler at me." Mali had said to her while reaching out to give her a hug. "Yo Shay, is my wife good, baby girl? Is everything okay with her?" He asked her while looking puzzled and confused about her unexpected pop up visit.

Shay was shocked when Mali asked her how Stephanie was doing, she'd never known of him to acknowledge his main in public, especially in front of his slider crew.

"Yeah bruh, she good but you know that's not what I came here to talk with you about." Shay had told him while folding both of her arms and staring directly at him.

Shay looked at Mali and hunched her head to the side. "Do you want to go to my car so we can talk in private?" She had asked him with a look of sincerity on her face.

"Yea, I got somewhere we can go talk at, it's cool shorty." Mali had told her while escorting her towards the gas station's store.

Mali had told Shay that they could go talk in the back of the store inside of the gas station for privacy. He led her through the gas station store to a small back room where they were able to talk.

Before they reached the back room of the gas station, an Arab gentleman with a heavy accent had yelled something out to Mali.

"Mali, now brother what in the hell are you doing with that woman?" The store owner had yelled out to him. "What about Stephanie, your new wife, my friend?" The store owner had asked him while following him and Shay towards the back of the store.

"Mali, you can't come up in here with that shit no more my man, I need for you to take your freaks the hell up out of my store right now, my friend." The store owner had told him as he continued to follow Mali and Shay to the back of the store.

Mali stopped in his tracks to turn around and laugh out loud at the store's owner. Mali was holding his tummy as he laughed and chuckled at the store's owner for his misconception of him and Shay.

"Aye yo calm down baby, you gon' stress yourself out Ali, this here is Shay, my wife's best friend, and my little sister man." Mali had explained to him while as they made their way towards the back room.

"Well yea mother fucker, I'm just trying to make sure that you do the right thing, you cheat on Stephanie mother fucker for one of these crumbs I'm going to kill you personally myself." Ali had told him before leaving to head back up front.

Unbeknownst to Shay, Mali had made a pact with his boys in the hood about a year ago that he had quit the game and laid his mac hand down. Mali had also told his boys that if he dogged out his wife or even played her ever again, he would pay up $50,000 to whoever caught him breaking her heart or cheating.

Mali had figured that Shay wanted to speak with him in regards to Cherry getting herself locked up in federal prison since she'd never mentioned anything to him about it before. Mali had further figured that since Shay found out about him and Stephanie being engaged, it was time for them to finally talk. Mali hadn't paid much attention to Cherry and Shay's friendship towards one another, nor had he cared, for all that he could have known, Cherry and Shay were still best friends.

One thing that Mali could count on for sure was for Shay to keep her big mouth shut when it came down to his private and personal business. Mali was aware that Shay knew of his deepest and darkest secrets, but he never had to worry about her ever saying a thing. When Shay had noticed that Mali was the prince whom Stephanie had always referred to as her fiancé, she was in total shock and disbelief at dinner that night.

When Stephanie introduced Mali to everyone at dinner, Shay had acted as if she had never known of Mali. In Mali's eyes, Shay wasn't a hater, he looked at her as a little sister who always blackmailed him and bribed him into buying her just about anything.

Mali and Shay had practically grown up together since he had been best friends with her older cousin since grade school. Mali had basically watched Shay grow up from a little girl at the age of six years old. Mali and Shay had a strange brother-sister connection that no one outside of their family had known about.

Mali and Shay's older cousin had taught Shay about being loyal to her family first, and never to the streets. They had both known that Shay had dated a lot of different dudes from

hood and was always out and about running her mouth {

in someone else business. They used Shay and her big mouth to

their advantage and made sure that she always came to them and

reported any and everything that she heard in the streets period.

Shay had always kept Mali and her older cousin one step ahead of

the game, they had always known about any and everything that

was going on around them.

Mali had felt that whatever it was that Shay had come to talk

with him about that afternoon for sure wasn't pertaining him or

Stephanie. Mali had figured to himself, that if Shay had any

questions about his and Stephanie's relationship she would for sure

come to him first regarding any matter.

Once Ali had left from out of the back of the store to let Mali and

Shay talk in private, Shay couldn't hold her anxiety in anymore,

she had begun blurting out all types of shit to Mali without ever

second-guessing.

"Do you honestly truly love Stephanie, Mali?" Shay had

boldly asked him with a look of concern and confusion on her face.

Mali had looked at Shay in her face as if she had lost her last mind by questioning him about how he loved his wife. Mali had

thought to himself for a brief moment, yo what the fuck is wrong

with   Shay if this lonely ass bitch doesn't go find herself some

business to get into.

"Yo, what in the hell are you talking about Shay? Girl don't

come up in my spot questioning me about how I love and feel for

my wife." Mali had sarcastically said towards her. "What kind of

drugs are you fucking with baby girl, asking me some foul sour ass

shit like this." Mali had asked her with anger and hostility in his

voice.

Mali had figured that out of all of the people that he had

known, Shay should have known him the best. Mali had felt that if

he had cut anyone off for any woman, he for sure ass hell had to

have love for her unconditionally.

Shay hadn't intended for Mali to get upset with her so quickly,

and she couldn't find the right words to say to him that evening to

help him calm down. "I'm sorry Mali, I honestly didn't mean to

make you upset, bruh." Shay had mumbled to him underneath her

breath while shyly looking away.

Shay had decided that now was a good time to go into detail

with Mali and explain to him how she had run into Liz at the mall
about a month ago.

"Mali, I saw one of your old flings Liz in the mall a little
while back, and you no me Mali, you know how I am and you
know how I was raised." Shay had explained to him. "Instead of
me going to Steph about the situation Mali, I had come straight to
you first despite that Stephanie is my best friend." Shay had
explained to him, still trying to apologize for her assumption and
outburst earlier.

Shay had told Mali everything that Liz had told her about
being pregnant for him with his first baby when she had seen her at
the mall last month.

Mali was furious once Shay had filled him in on everything
that Liz had lied to her about. Mali didn't want to get angry or
upset in front of Shay because he knew how Shay was with her big
ass mouth. Instead, Mali had tried to keep his cool with Shay. He
had already known from past experience, that if he let Shay see
him get upset or angry, she would run back and tell Liz everything
that he was going to do to her out of hate and anger on Liz's end.

Mali couldn't believe what Liz was going around saying about him. He had thought to himself, how could this bitch make up some crazy foul ass bullshit like this about me?

Mali explained to Shay that he hadn't spoken with Liz or any of his other side bitches in almost a year or so now. He had further gone to explain to her that once he hooked up with Cherry and introduced her to the game, she had run circles around Liz and her crew when it had come to busting moves and scheming for the money. Mali told Shay that Cherry alone was bringing in ten times more money than Liz or any of her girls have ever done alone. He explained to Shay that Cherry was hungry and ready to impress him by any means necessary.

"Yo baby girl, Cherry did herself in, she was too ready to pay the kid." Mali had told her while bragging about how much money Cherry had brought him in. Mali had begun to get excited with himself when he reminisced about all of the money that Cherry had helped him make.

Mali had explained to Shay how he advised Cherry and her team to slow down on their movement. He had told Shay that once Cherry and her girls had got a taste of making some real bands, she had begun to get greedy and felt like she no longer had to listen to him anymore. Mali had gone into detail explaining to Shay that once Cherry turned her back on him and started getting cocky and big headed, he had felt as if she had no longer needed him since she had no longer listened to a word that he had said anyway.

Mali told Shay that he left Cherry to hang herself, due to her disrespecting him and the game. He explained to Shay how he put Cherry up on game when it came to making some real money, and that she had felt the urge to suddenly turn her back on him and get big headed.

"Shay, that bitch even went as far as trying to move her and her grandmother up out of the hood to the top of the Skyline hill, mind you, the scandalous shady ass bitch didn't know me and my wife both had houses on that same fucking hill." Mali had said to her. "Shay you know damn well you're never supposed to bite the hand that feeds you, the game god will always eventually come back to get you." Mali told Shay, leaning against the table fuming mad and pissed off with just the thought of Cherry.

Shay stood in the back of the store in shock from everything that she had just heard about   Cherry. Shay had no idea of what had actually gone on between the two. Shay had known from the way that Mali had explained his story, it was the total truth. Shay had known how Cherry was, and she knew how Mali was as well. Shay had known how Cherry could get when given the opportunity to make herself some real money. Shay knew Cherry most likely hung herself out to dry with catching her federal case.

The whole time Shay was in contact with Mrs. Green, she and Cherry made it look as if something completely different had taken place between her and Mali. Maybe that's why Cherry ran her grandmother away from me, Shay had thought to herself. Shay had refused to go into detail or even say anything to Mali about the lies that Cherry and Mrs. Green had said to her about him. Shay had known that if she mentioned a word to Mali about Cherry and Mrs. Green, it would open up an unwanted can of worms. Shay felt her loyalty was with Stephanie, and that was the main reason she came to see him.

"Shay, it was just a matter of time before Cherry got herself caught up with the Feds." Mali had told her with a look of pity and concern in his face. "I tried to tell her, baby girl, that she was moving way to fast, but you know your best friend, she didn't listen." Mali said to Shay while folding both of his arms.

Mali went into further detail with Shay, explaining to her that Cherry and her team was clearing out more than $2 million dollars every other month in just merchandise alone. Once Liz had found out that Cherry and her team was bringing in $500,000 every other month, she immediately called herself leaving.

Mali went into detail explaining to Shay that he and Liz never had sex before. He told Shay that Liz could go out and have all of the kids she wanted to, but he for sure could never be any of their fathers.

"Baby girl I wouldn't even waste my time taking that bitch to the Maury show, I would for sure win, but I'm not into calling much attention to myself at all." Mali had told her before laughing to himself out loud. "Shay, I would even go as far as paying for the bitch a DNA test right now, we don't have to wait for the baby to be born." He arrogantly said.

Mali began to laugh in Shay's face with the news that she had brought to his attention about Liz. He shook his head at Shay before telling her, "It's gold down their baby girl, everything that glitters ain't what you want ma', and you should even know better than that." Mali said.

"They work harder for you baby girl when you don't give them any of your gold fairy dust." He arrogantly told her before getting up from off of the table to walk out of the room to leave.

Mali was cocky, and it showed. He felt disrespect by Shay even approaching him with some he say she say bullshit about Liz. Mali turned around to look at Shay and waved his hand for her to come on and leave with him.

"Baby girl, I thought you knew your big brother better than that ma." He had arrogantly said to her as they walked out of the gas station store to leave.

CHAPTER NINE

Liz was home running her mouth on the phone talking with one of her homegirls about a whole bunch of nothing. She was complaining and whining to one of her friends about how tired and sorry her baby daddy was. Liz was getting herself ready to head out of the door for her two-month prenatal checkup.

"Hold up girl let me call you back later on, so I can hurry up and get myself together before I end up being late to my doctor's appointment." She told her friend before disconnecting the call. Liz had run around her apartment, gathering up the last few of her things before heading out of her front door to leave that morning.

Liz had made her way out to the front of her carport on the opposite side of her apartment building. She had noticed, that once she made it to the carport, her 2013 Mercedes Benz CL 500 wasn't parked where she had left it.

Before Liz began to panic she had checked around her carport, thinking to herself that she had parked it in a different space. After walking around her carport two separate times, she stopped to think to herself that maybe her baby daddy had stolen her keys and took her car without her permission.

Liz brushed off the thought about her baby daddy once she had noticed that she still had her car keys in her hand. Liz changed her attention away from her baby daddy and towards someone hating on her and stealing her car from her instead.

Liz figured to herself that she did have the fliest car that was out in her new neighborhood. She had figured that ever since she relocated her housing and moved into her new project unit in the burbs, everyone in the jets had started hating on her for no reason. None of the females in Liz's new apartment complex liked her or her expensive way of project living. Liz figured that everyone was jealous of her fly, flashy, expensive lifestyle, and they needed to start getting used to it.

When Liz had finally decided to call the police and report her car stolen that morning, she had remembered that Mali had all of the information and paperwork to the Mercedes. Liz couldn't even verify the license plate number over the phone to the police dispatch whom she was speaking with. Liz was so damn dumb that she never took the time out to write anything down in regards to the Mercedes Benz.

When Mali had originally given Liz her Benz about a year or so ago, he never gave her any of the paperwork or the registration to the vehicle. Liz had always just assumed that the Mercedes was rightfully hers since Mali had never tried to come back and take it from her.

Liz was so wrapped up in her own thoughts and ways, that she never suspected Mali of taking her vehicle at all. Liz was so full of herself until she focused all of her attention on her neighbors, claiming that everyone was hating on her and wishing her bad from the very first day that she had moved in. Liz had figured to herself that if Mali wanted to take her car back, he could have done so months ago before she had moved out of her old unit in the sixty-fifth village.

Liz was frustrated and tired of herself since she wasn't able to make it to her doctor's appointment that morning. She was even more pissed off because someone had stolen her car. Liz refused to call Mali for help knowing that he hadn't been dealing with her in the first place.

Mali pulled up to the gas station, where he and his boys were known to hang out at on Seminary and MacArthur, in Liz's 2013 Mercedes Benz CL 500. When Mali had pulled up to the gas station in Liz's Benz, some of his boys were over in the corner wilding out playing in a dice game. Mali rolled his passenger side window down and called over for one of his boys to come and take a ride with him. One of his boys who was just standing around quickly ran over to the Mercedes Benz and hopped in.

Mali had driven off from the gas station with his boy close by his side. He had handed his boy a handful of weed and some swisher sweets and asked him to roll up while they took a ride. Mali's boy had taken the weed and did as Mali had asked him to while Mali drove to the paint shop to sell Liz's old Mercedes Benz. Mali had filled his boy in on everything that was going on with Liz while he continued to drive. He had explained to his boy the reason for taking back Liz's Benz and selling it. Mali and his boy continued to engage in small talk as they weaved in and out of traffic while smoking on a blunt.

"Yo that's some foul ass fucked up shit that bitch did to you B, why can't these hoes ever be satisfied with whatever type of nigga they get yo." Mali's boy had said to him. "It's like these bitches be too damn picky nowadays when it comes to a nigga." His boy had told him.

"Man bruh, when will these bitches ever learn yo, take what you can get ma, especially if it's a good ass nigga." Mali's boy had said to him while choking off of the weed. "Yo, this here is some fire ass dro big bra, where in the fuck did you get this here shit from?" His boy had asked him while taking another pull from the blunt before passing him the weed. "Yo better yet, where in the fuck are we going to, my nigga?" His boy asked him, tripping off of the high from the weed.

Mali's boy was tripping off of his weed high so hard that he had kept asking Mali the same thing over and over again, Mali had already answered his question by explaining to him earlier when he had first got into the car about where it was that they were going.

"We going to the paint shop fool, yo bra you need to lay up off of all of that weed! Your memory is straight shit blud." Mali had told his boy while laughing out loud as they pulled in front of the paint shop.

Mali and his boy had pulled into the paint shop as they both jumped out of the Mercedes with a cloud full of weed smoke trailing close behind them. Mali walked ahead of his boy in search of the owner of the auto body shop, while his boy followed close behind him doing the same thing.

"Mali my boy, where have you been?" The owner of the shop had asked him while extending his hand out to it shake while also greeting him. The owner was in the back of the auto body shop inside of his office doing some paperwork when Mali and his boy had walked in.

"So are you 100% for sure that you want to sell me this here Mercedes Benz?" The owner had asked him while pointing to Liz's Benz parked out front. "Now Mali, you say you bought this here car what, three years or so ago right?" The owner had asked Mali while looking at him to make sure that he was sure of what he was doing.

"Yea, everything is all good baby." Mali had told him, eager to get rid of the Mercedes Benz.

Alright then Mali, it sounds like a deal my friend." the owner had told him while extending his hand once again to out shake and agree to their deal.

The owner had escorted Mali and his boy to his office towards the back of his shop, where they could further discuss business.

Just as Mali and his boy were about to sit down and have a seat, the owner quickly changed his mind on where it was that they would be meeting.

"You know what Mali, I want for you two gentlemen to follow me out back instead." The owner had told them while escorting Mali and his friend out of his office and outback towards the back of the building.

Mali and his boy followed the shop's owner close behind, without saying a word or asking any questions. When the trio reached the back of the building outside, they had gone into a second office room that was more secluded away from any and everyone.

The office was outside in the back of the body shop, inside of what seemed to look like an office shed. Once the owner had unlocked the door with his keys, he had then stepped to the side and invited Mali and his boy inside.

Once everyone was inside of the back office, the owner had then gone over to his desk to retrieve a large envelope. The envelope was filed away in his desk drawer with a bunch of other papers. The owner retrieved the envelope and handed it over to Mali.

Mali took the envelope from the shop's owner and inspected the package before telling his boy to close the door while he had opened it up.

Once Mali had opened up the manila envelope, he had noticed that it contained a stack of the auto body shop customers personal profiles. He had further looked through the stack of profiles to notice there was a personal check written out to Stephanie in the amount of $20,000.

Mali had known that the stack of profiles was worth way more than the Mercedes he was selling, he had known that he could bring in more money than the car was actually worth.

Mali figured since Liz wanted to run around and start running her mouth and lying months before his wedding, he would just stoop down to her level and take back his Mercedes.

At first, he wasn't going to bother her about the Mercedes at all, he had figured that since she had already had the car he would let her keep it so that she could go on about her life and leave him alone. Since Liz wanted to go around and run her mouth starting shit, he took the car knowing that she wouldn't be able to run around yapping her mouth without a car to get around in.

Fuck that foul ass bitch, Mali had thought to himself. Mali had figured that he had been more than nice to Liz since he still allowed her to keep the Mercedes Benz after he wasn't fucking with her at all anymore.

"That's what I get for being nice to a bum ass bitch!" He had silently yelled out to himself. Mali had begun to get upset just by thinking of Liz trying to upset Stephanie.

Mali had thought that by allowing Liz to keep the Mercedes she would stay out of his face and away from Stephanie, and she still couldn't do that right. He had figured that since Liz wanted to play dirty with him and kick up a bunch of bullshit, he would do the same with her and take back his Benz.

After Mali verified everything in the envelope, the owner had walked him and his boy back to the front of the shop, where he had a custom painted candy apple red 1970 Chevrolet Chevelle SS 427 LS6 waiting on him. Mali had previously placed his Chevelle in the paint shop weeks before planning to take back Liz's Mercedes

Benz.

Mali had shaken the owner's hand as him and his boy had hopped in his custom Chevelle, and revved up the engine, and headed back towards the gas station with the rest of his friends.

Liz had sat at home looking dumbfounded in the face, upset with the fact that someone had stolen her Mercedes Benz. She had sat at home on the phone, calling anyone and everyone that was willing to listen to her explain to them how someone was hating on her in her apartment complex and had stolen her Benz.

Liz couldn't believe that she was without a whip, and didn't have a clue as to who could have stolen it. Liz had never once questioned herself as to why she never had any of the paperwork to the Mercedes in the first place considering that it was "her car." When it came to Liz handling her own personal business, she didn't have any common sense.

Liz was a hustler, and she had already known what it was that she was going to have to do in order to maintain her reputation and uphold her personal image. Liz had figured to herself that she could no longer afford to have a baby without a car for her to get around in.

Liz had felt that in order for her to maintain her reputation, she was going to have to go into hustle mode. She had felt that whoever took her Mercedes Benz would never have the chance to have the last laugh and make her look like a fool. Liz had figured that if anyone would be laughing, it would be her all the way to the bank in her brand new 2015 BMW X6. Liz had told herself that if she hustled ten times harder and flip a brand new whip off of the car lot ten times better than the car that she had already had, she would still be on top.

Instead of Liz living in reality and fantasizing about a decent living with proper employment, she dreamed of owning a fly ride and busting major money licks. Liz envisioned herself as being that bitch in the hood, Liz had felt that she was a hood superstar and the ghetto's trap Queen. Liz felt like the definition of living life was no further than a few out of state plane rides and the Oakland city streets.

Weeks had gone past and Liz had begun to get over the fact that she no longer had her Mercedes Benz. She had also come to realize that she had no real true friends. When Liz had her Mercedes, she sided with everyone so hard until they had eventually turned their backs on her.

Liz was stressing for some money, and she wanted to maintain her reputation and image so badly that she started running around busting fraudulent checks as her new get rich quick scheme. Liz had hooked up with one of her old male friends from back in the day, who she once used to get money with before hooking up with Mali. The dude that Liz was busting her checks with was the first person who had ever laced her up on game when it had come to white-collar crime and busting fraud moves.

On Friday morning, Liz had decided that she was going to go out the night before and make herself some extra money by hitting a few moves.

That morning, Liz had run around from bank to bank trying her luck with busting her fraudulent checks. She had become so frustrated with herself that morning, seeming that she kept coming up with no luck, until she had decided to pull out her phone and call Mali.

At first, Liz hesitated on calling him, fearing that Shay had already spread word about her bashed pregnancy. Liz had decided to swallow her pride and call Mali anyway. She had begun to pick up her phone and dial his phone number after first pressing star sixty-seven to block out her phone number.

Liz knew that Mali's hustle was way easier and a lot more lucrative than what she was doing with the fraudulent checks. She had known that if she hooked back up with Mali, she wouldn't have to do half of the work she was doing now, nor take as many risks and chances. Just as Liz was about to press talk and send out her call to Mali, she had suddenly changed her mind and decided not to call him after all. Liz had figured to herself that she would try to contact him later on in the day after she tried to bust a few more moves to come up with a little more money. Liz had further figured to herself, that instead of approaching Mali empty handed and begging for a handout, she would come at him correct with a cool loaf of cash to start up on her own with him. Liz had wanted to make enough money to buy her own work from Mali, and she had felt that she no longer needed to work for him.

Liz sat in a small crowded clinic in Downtown San Pablo as she read a magazine, while patiently waiting for her name to be called out by one of the clinic's nurses. She had been waiting for one of the nurses to call out her name for over two and a half hours now, and she still wasn't close to being seen.

Just as Liz was about to get frustrated and blow up on one of

the nurses, someone was yelling out her name from one of the back

rooms.

Liz got up from her seat and head over towards the nurse who

was calling her name, who was standing by the door waiting to let

her in. Liz had slightly walked over to the nurse from carrying the

weight of her now three-month-old baby. The nurse escorted her to

a back room, where she has advised Liz to get undressed.

The nurse had later told Liz that the doctor would be in shortly

to see her and closed the door behind her as Liz begins to get

undressed in the small room. Liz had undressed while she waited

for the doctor to come in. Liz laid flat on her back across the

surgical table as she waited for the doctor to come into the room to

complete her procedure.

Liz laid across the abortion table with a million thoughts going

through her head. She hadn't known the real reason as to why she

had waited so long to have her abortion done in the first place. And

Liz had refused to give birth to a baby that was by anyone other

than Mali. She had already figured to herself that if Mali wasn't going to be able to be the father of her baby, then no one else would.

It was now two days after Liz has had her abortion, and she was already out back at it busting check licks all over again. It was towards the end of spring, and it was a nice day to be out. Liz had started out the day doing pretty good for herself, although she was heavily bleeding.

Liz was in a lot of pain from her abortion, and she continued to do what she had to do far as making herself some money. Liz wasn't letting anything or anyone stop her from getting her dough.

It was only twelve noon, and Liz had already made nearly $9,000 in cash. Liz could have easily quit and given up for the day, but she had a goal to meet. Liz had told herself that morning that champions take chances, and quitters never win. She had plans on meeting her goal of $20,000 a day, and by any means, she was going to get it.

Liz had figured that she could impress Mali with buying her own work from him and by approaching him with $50,000 in cash and still having a cool amount in her personal stash. Liz had figured that before she could approach Mali with the $50,000 in cash, she would first have to buy herself a new, fly, foreign whip to pull up on him in.

Liz drove down the highway looking for her next exit, blasting her music strategizing on her next bank move. She had noticed that on her phone's bank app there was another bank only two miles away towards the direction that she was headed. Liz had floored the gas pedal of her 1999 Mazda 626, feeling excited with luck all in the air that was around her. She made her way towards her exit and pulled into the bank's parking lot.

Liz didn't think twice about going into the bank as she parked her car before grabbing a few of her papers, and making her way inside.

Liz was standing in line at the bank, on her cell phone talking to one of her homegirls and running her mouth about nothing in particular. She was on the phone with one of her homegirls trying to decide on where it was that they were going to go to go out and eat and have dinner later on that night. Liz was running her mouth so much on the phone, that she hadn't noticed that she was drawing extra unwanted attention to herself. In fact, Liz hadn't noticed that the bank manager had interest in her phone conversation and whatever else it was that she had planned on doing inside of his bank that day. The manager of the bank had decided that whatever it was that Liz was coming inside of his bank to do, it was going to have to go through him first.

CHAPTER TEN

Stephanie and Shay were out enjoying themselves in Dubai with a few of their other family members and close friends. Not only had Shay come along with Stephanie, but her cousin Desmond and her older sister Lisa had also come along as planned. Although Desmond came at Stephanie's expense, she was still grateful to have him there.

Everyone was out enjoying themselves horseback riding and sight-seeing with their tour guide through the white sands of Dubai, without a care in the world.

Meanwhile, Stephanie had stayed back at her hotel room preparing herself for a date that she had planned with a new friend that she had recently met in Dubai the night before. Stephanie had encouraged everyone else on her trip to go ahead and enjoy the rest of their tour for the day without her.

Stephanie had told everyone that she had received an urgent email from her office back home and that she had unexpected work to tend to. Stephanie had told Shay to let everyone else know that she would catch up with them, later on, that night at dinner.

Stephanie had met her new friend the night after she checked into her hotel room while standing in the hotel lobby. He was a Peruvian gentleman with a cocoa almond skin complexion. He had a sleek physique with an enticing body.

The Peruvian man had sat in the hotel lobby watching Stephanie from the opposite side of the room as she spoke with the hotel's concierge. She was speaking with the concierge about a few of the afternoon tours that she had already planned. The gentleman on the opposite side of the hotel room had overheard their conversation through the echo of the hotel's lobby and had decided then to approach Stephanie as she was still speaking with the concierge.

"Excuse me miss." The gentleman had spoken to her with a thick Arabic accent. He had first excused himself from interrupting the hotel's concierge and had then turned his attention back towards Stephanie. He held out his hand towards Stephanie to greet her like a proper gentleman.

"Miss, unfortunately, I was admiring your beauty from the opposite side of the room without your permission, please do forgive me for my wicked stare." He had told her while holding her hand inside of his before lifting it up to his lips to place a kiss on the back of it. Stephanie was lost for words, she had no idea of what to say as she had started to blush in front of him.

The gentleman had noticed that he had grasped Stephanie's attention from the kiss on the back of her hand, and he had continued to compliment her on the way that she had looked that night. He had caught Stephanie off guard by asking her if she would allow him to escort her to lunch the very next day. Stephanie was flattered with the approach of the gentleman, and she was intrigued with his boldness.

Stephanie had first thought about telling the gentleman that she was on vacation for her bridal shower and that she couldn't accept his offer to lunch because she was already engaged to someone else. But before she could open her mouth and get her thoughts together, she had unknowingly accepted his offer.

"Of course, I would be delighted to get better acquainted with you tomorrow afternoon during lunch." Stephanie had blurted out to him while staring into his eyes with a seductive smile.

The gentleman had met Stephanie in the middle of the hotel lobby that afternoon for lunch as they had planned the night before. He had greeted her with a dozen long-stem white roses that were placed neatly inside of a white box that was lined with silk paper lining.

The stems of the roses were bunched close together inside of the box, with a bright fluorescent pink bow placed in the center of them. Stephanie had begun to get butterflies in her stomach as she accepted the box of roses from him. Stephanie was able to smell the scent of his cologne lingering in the box of roses.

The gentleman had escorted Stephanie out of the hotel towards the front, where a Phantom Rolls Royce awaited for the both of them at the hotel's front entrance. The driver had greeted them both as he escorted Stephanie by the hand into the back of the car. The gentleman had eagerly followed close behind her before the driver had closed the door to walk himself to the opposite side of the car.

The driver had then pulled away from the hotel as the gentleman had given him specific instructions in a foreign language as to where it was that they were supposed to be going to. After giving the driver their location, he had then turned his attention back towards Stephanie. He looked her deep in the eyes, promising her that she would have the time of her life with him while she was on her trip in Dubai.

Once they had arrived at the villa that afternoon for lunch, Stephanie was amazed by the atmosphere as well as the view.

They examined each other with seductive stares in their eyes as they enjoyed their meals together. They had exotic and strange feelings for each other that made them both want to be near one another more and more that afternoon. Before lunch was over, he had asked Stephanie if he could take her out once again before she had left Dubai.

The gentleman had escorted Stephanie back to her hotel room later on that evening after they had enjoyed their lunch. He kissed her softly on both of her lips before turning away to leave her room. Before he made his way down the hallway towards the elevator, he stopped and remembered that he had never told her his name.

"By the way, Stephanie." The gentleman had yelled out to her as he made his way down the hall. "You never once bothered to ask me my name, and yet I know so much about you." He had told her before walking towards the elevator. "Stephanie, my name is Ali, and I'm pleased to meet you." He had said to her as he stepped onto the hotel's elevator.

Stephanie had opened her hotel room door, amazed at the way that Ali had treated her while they were out on their date for lunch that evening. She had stumbled into her room tipsy from her cocktails that afternoon and laid her box of roses across her hotel bed. She had begun to sit on her bed and remove her shoes, just as she had noticed that her message light was blinking red.

Shay had called Stephanie's cell phone and room phone continuously with no luck of getting anyone to answer.

"So let me guess." Desmond stated to her while popping his lips and placing both of his hands on his hips. "She still not answering neither one of them phones, and you mean to tell me that Y'all just gon' sit here and keep calling, hoping that eventually, someone answers it?" Desmond told Shay while rolling his eyes at her and turning to walk away.

"I bet that fool done ran off with some random ass nigga, months before her wedding day." Desmond had told them while flopping onto Shay's hotel bed.

"Hold on now Desmond, you're taking it too damn far." Shay had told him while pointing her finger at him from across the room. "Let's not start jumping to conclusions here, alright Desmond? Stephanie's a whole grown ass woman. I'm pretty sure she knows what she's doing out here." Shay had told him.

"Let's just all go ahead and go out to dinner without her, I'm sure that she knows how to find us since she did plan this whole trip in the first place." Shay had told everyone while preparing to leave for dinner that night.

"Whatever Shay." Desmond had told her while fanning his hands in front of her face and picking up his things.

Desmond and Shay continued to argue back and forth with each other about Stephanie's well being and her whereabouts that night. They had yelled and bickered with one another about who had the right to tell who what it was that they needed to do next. Despite all of Desmond and Shay's bickering back and forth with one another, Lisa had decided to call the hotel's concierge and advise him that they were ready to leave and would be coming down soon.

The room had gone silent as soon as the hotel phone rang. "I'll get it." Desmond had yelled out while rolling his eyes at Shay and switching his hips side to side. Desmond had answered the phone on the second ring while Lisa and the rest of the girls had finished gathering up their purses to head out of the door for dinner. "Hello, Desmond speaking." Desmond had stated to the concierge in a soft seductive tone.

"Your car is ready ma'am," the concierge had told him before disconnecting the line.

"Okay, why thank you so much, sir." Desmond said while smiling through the phone, happy that the concierge had referred to him as ma'am instead of sir.

Desmond hung up the phone cheerful and buttery with the words from the concierge, happy he wasn't referred to as a man. Everyone fell out laughing once they had all turned around and noticed Desmond doing his little happy dance.

Stephanie was having the time of her life in Dubai, and she

had felt as if she was being treated like a Queen. Although Mali treated her good back at home, he had never treated her the way that Ali had done. Stephanie had only envisioned this type of treatment from a man inside of her dreams, or inside of a good book. She had never expected to receive this type of treatment from any man in reality.

Stephanie had spent her time in Dubai away from her family and friends that had come along with her to celebrate her bridal shower. Instead, she had explained to everyone that she had met a friend in Dubai and that she wanted to spend as much time with him that she could before they had all headed back home to the US. With everyone knowing the way Stephanie was when it came to her and men, they all agreed to continue the rest of their vacation in Dubai without her being with them.

Stephanie's date had arrived at her hotel room to escort her out on their second date thirty minutes early, that evening and she was caught off guard due to his early arrival that afternoon. Stephanie was still in the bathtub preparing herself to get ready for dinner when he had entered her room. Ali had come through the door with a spare room key that Stephanie had given him a few days before.

"Sweetheart, are you almost properly prepared for this afternoon?" Ali had yelled out to her from the front of her hotel room. Ali had stood in front of a wall mirror by the entrance of the hotel door, admiring himself and adjusting the cufflinks on his suit.

Stephanie had hopped out of the bathtub and walked over to the bedroom dripping wet once she had noticed that Ali had arrived. She hadn't bothered grabbing herself a bath towel once she left out of the bathroom since she was running late. Stephanie walked over to her suitcase with bath bubbles falling off of her naked body and had begun pulling out random outfits to wear. She had started to get excited with herself for no apparent reason, and began dancing and prancing around the room trying on different outfits.

Most of the men that Stephanie had dated were American black men, and they had never catered to her the way that Ali did. Stephanie had never dated outside of her race, however, she had looked at Ali a lot differently from the way that she had looked at American men.

Stephanie greeted Ali at the front entrance of her hotel room once she was dressed and prepared to leave. Ali had patiently waited for her by the front entrance of her hotel door, with a dozen long stem white roses as always when he had come to take her out for a date. Stephanie had accepted her gift, and sat the box of roses on the front table in the lounge area of her hotel room as they prepared to head out of the door for their dinner date that afternoon.

Ali was a real gentleman towards Stephanie, and he had wanted nothing more from her than to show her a good time while she was out in Dubai with her friends and family. He had wanted to show her the other side of the world and what she was missing and needing to see. Ali had briefly interrupted Stephanie from her daydream during dinner by asking her a question.

"Stephanie my love, are you okay?" he asked her while wiping his mouth with a cloth napkin to assure that he didn't spit out any food towards her way. "It seems to me that something is bothering you, my love." Ali had questioned her in a seductive Arabic accent.

"Yes, Ali I'm fine." Stephanie had muttered out to him before taking a sip of her red wine.

Stephanie was falling in love with Ali and she wanted to stay in Dubai to be with him forever. Although she was engaged and about to marry Mali once she had returned back home, she had wanted to call it quits and call off their whole wedding.

Ali had made her feel like no other man had ever done in her life before, and she wanted to keep that sensual, genuine, dedicated, and devoted feeling. And Ali had also felt the same way for Stephanie, from the very first day that he had laid eyes on her in their hotel lobby.

Stephanie was blind to the type of man that Ali really was, she had no idea of his financial importance, and for that reason it made Ali want her even more.

Most of the tourists that came out to Dubai on their vacations to visit came just for the chance to see Ali. Stephanie, on the other hand, had never really done any of her homework, so therefore she knew nothing personally about her new friend. Stephanie hadn't known that she was the lucky one in a million women who had an actual chance of being in the presence of an Arabian prince.

Stephanie had enjoyed the rest of her vacation in Dubai without ever returning to her room, or without any of her family members or friends.

Stephanie had called Shay to let her no that everyone's entire vacation had been paid for in full, including their airfare and hotel rooms. She had further advised Shay that there was a sudden change in her plans, Stephanie had felt that this would be the best way to accommodate them for her being absent on their trip and leaving.

Stephanie had also informed Shay that they would be checking out of their hotel rooms early and that someone would be coming to pick them up from the front to escort them over to the exquisite Address Hotel, Downtown Dubai.

Everyone was so excited with the news that Shay had given them that morning that they immediately jumped up from breakfast and did as told without asking any questions or without any hesitation.

Even Desmond was excited to hear what he had just heard, he was even more anxious to see what Stephanie had in store for them next. Since Stephanie always had a trick up her sleeve, no one complained or questioned her about anything. Stephanie had left everyone that morning, advising them that she would meet up with them again at the airport within the next week when they were all scheduled to leave.

Lisa and Shay, along with everyone else on their trip, assumed that Mali had flown out to Dubai to be with Stephanie while they were on vacation, especially with considering all of the amenities that they were all now enjoying for free.

Everyone had continued to enjoy their time in Dubai without Stephanie being present, never questioning her whereabouts. Everyone had just kept assuming that she was out enjoying Dubai with Mali somewhere, being romantic before their big wedding.

Everyone met up at the airport as scheduled the following week, excepting to see Stephanie with Mali.

"Where's Mali at, Steph?" Desmond had asked her as they stood in line to go through customs clearance. Desmond swung his carry-on bag back and forth between his legs while he waited for Stephanie to answer him.

"Desmond, you know damn well that Mali didn't come out here with us on this trip, stop being stupid." She had told him while rolling her eyes at him, frustrated with his annoying question. Desmond's mouth dropped wide open, and his eyes grew big as bow dollars when he had heard Stephanie say that she wasn't with Mali on their trip. Desmond dropped his bags and turned towards the other girls as he pretended to faint and sip tea with Stephanie's news.

It had now been one month since Stephanie and Shay had been back from Dubai, and not once had Stephanie mentioned anything to Shay about planning for her wedding.

Their wedding was supposed to be scheduled within two months of them returning from Dubai, but Stephanie had never mentioned a thing. Before they had left for her bridal shower, they had made previous plans to come straight back home and finish up planning for her big wedding. Shay on the on the hand had figured that the whole point of them going to Dubai was for Stephanie's bridal shower, and not for her to have an epiphany about her personal life.

Shay had gone along with the flow of her best friend and had never questioned her or said a word to her about anything pertaining to her wedding.

Shay had begun to notice a change in Stephanie for the better, and she had noticed that Stephanie all of a sudden had a glow within herself that had shined brighter from within. Although Stephanie was already high maintenance, she now was coming into the office with custom-made Donatella Versace suits and Alexandre Herchcovitch shoes. Shay had also noticed that Stephanie had recently parked her Bentley GT that she had claimed to have loved so much, and had started driving a brand new custom 2014 Phantom Coupe. Engraved on the door panels it stated Exclusively Hand Built for Stephanie, One of One.

Stephanie hadn't mentioned anything to Shay about her and Mali canceling their wedding, or about her new friend in Dubai.

Shay knew that when it came to Stephanie's personal business, she better not have asked her any questions. If Stephanie hadn't mentioned it previously to her, Shay had known better than to ask her anything further. Shay had known from first-hand experience that if Stephanie felt you were digging around in her personal business, she would immediately cut you off and act as if she never met you and place you at a far distance. Shay continued to stay on Stephanie's good side until she decided to fill her in on what had been going on in her life.

"Shay, can I speak with you in private in my office please?"

Stephanie had asked her one morning while coming in for work.

"Yeah sure Steph, did you wish for me to come see you right now?" Shay had asked her nervously. Stephanie stopped in the middle of the hallway to turn around and look at Shay.

"Shay if you don't bring your black ass to my office right now girl." Stephanie had told her, breaking the tension and fear that Shay had felt. Shay logged off of her computer from emailing her children father on Corr Links and rushed over to meet up with Stephanie.

"Close the door behind you Shay." Stephanie had told her in a stern strict voice. Shay didn't know what to think or what was going on with Stephanie wanting to see her.

Normally when Stephanie had called for her to come to her office to meet up with her, it was usually for them to sip on some tea and gossip about other people's business. But this morning things were completely different for Shay and Stephanie, and Shay could tell from the look on Stephanie's face that she had meant business.

Stephanie had sat across from Shay with both of her hands folded on top of her desk and had told her best friend that she may have noticed there hadn't been any plans for her and Mali's wedding. She had also told Shay without going into any personal detail that the wedding had been postponed until further notice.

Shay's mouth had dropped, and from the look of frustration on Stephanie's face, Shay had known not to interrupt her or ask any questions.

Stephanie knew that Shay was nosy, and not only nosy but also messy and from Mali's hood. Stephanie had known that she couldn't confide in Shay about anything that was going on with her personal life because of her relationship with Mali and their close connection.

Stephanie knew that if she mentioned a word to Shay, it could get back to Mali and any of his personal groupies that she may decide to gossip with form their hood.

"Shay, I called you into my office to let you know that I'm going to personally need your assistance." Stephanie had told her while walking around the room and gathering up a few of her things, preparing to leave. "I'm going to be leaving out of the country in a few more hours on some very important business, and

I'm going to need for you to assist me with my emails and running the office." Stephanie had told her before handing her a set of office keys.

Shay didn't have a chance to ask Stephanie anything, all that Shay could do was sit back in her chair and look around as Stephanie walked around boxing up a few of her things. For once in Shay's life, she had become speechless and lost for words.

Skeemin On Tha Low 2